Narrow Doors
In Wide
Green Fields

Surrealists and Outsiders - 2019

Editor – RW Spryszak

Cover Image – "Magic Glove" by Rikki Ducornet

ISBN-13: 978-1-945334-07-8

Please note that in some case the size of the typeface has been altered to stay true to the spacing and intention of the poet. The occasional change is not your eyes.

Thrice Publishing is a 501(c)3, Not For Profit corporation registered in the state of Illinois.
We accept tax deductible contributions from readers, writers, activists, and individuals committed to support the small press universe. Please consider what it means to live in a world where the only outlets for alternative writers and artists are hard to find and marginalized. Won't you please consider, in these times, helping? Support the small press and its writers.

Thrice Publishing
PO Box 725114
Roselle, IL 60172

Or visit

www.thricepublishing.com

to help.

CONTENTS

Hieroglyphic Nomad
Paul McRandle

Antequara

Dolmen de Viera, the ancient subterranean passage through limestone strata, sinking deeper along lines of failure, dripping stalagmites the streaming egg colors of ochre, malachite, the fluid mineral, each writhing under the ink of eternity. We sink from Mesolithic to Paleolithic then rise fast through the ages drifting towards the Neolithic stones and out into daylight drinking in the Roman Baths, eating curse tablets. This time the voyage induces no nausea, but the dead rise with us among the moth casings of old images and digital gaps. Sightless, blinded by the past in a groping search as you photograph me before the gate, locked on this stone portal, this theater, this mirror. I looked for you at the cafe in the shade of the late afternoon, the humbled, stretched day of long flight. For when have we ever known respite, this humanity raised in *furia* across the Eurasian landmass striking down the population of Orleans in a genocidal slaughter that Romans quickly forgot? But here in Iberia under Roman guard, here in Phoenician harness before the Sea People's sails, here where the cannibalized remains of the first peoples of Europe bear out the horror that would visit for hundreds of thousands of years, aion, eternity without end of corpses beneath the eye of humankind. The dismembered Baptist revived in wax to visit your dreams, each vein of his neck dispensed with sadistic care, the pale notch of spine resting like a joint in the middle of all that flesh. So strange to travel these strata, these images that cannot be undone, histories, amber blocks of duration floating and charged. You raise a hand among the rain drops to touch water adrift for centuries. Maybe it bears the oral records, the sounds of forgotten languages gliding in brownian motion ready to be divined with a dowsing rod and spoken by those anointed with rain. We are saturated now in a confusion of the past that sits over the bones of ideologies and mocks science. We are alone together with our contemporaries Torquemada, Stalin, and Caesar. This is the least certain of times when the genes in our veins shift with the quickening of gamma rays striking our planet from the depths outside. For what is it but the great outside, the further out of doors beyond which the Astral gods fume with indignant radiation. Their influence is felt, surely, even if the moon turns green just for me, just for her. We drop ourselves in bed and glide over the old maps and spaces that smell of blind water channels and sing with the whisper of bats.

Seville

In the gallery of used prestige we walk past the cat in the trees, back ridged and eyes lit with twilight, through gardens and among fountains cycling thought to thought, the alchemical circulation within the philosopher's egg meet the wry eye of the feline. A knockwurst hangs by its neck above a bar, jaunty drinkers saluting its writhings and twistings above their heads. What of it? There are peculiar goings on in this gallery. Wreckless speed for weak passengers hoping to get home unmolested aboard the autobus. We have fine divisions of makeshift things that coincides with the temporary, the ephemeral, the evanescent, the transitory, and the phantasmatic. Last but not least the eternal slips over the transom to wander the streets on velvety padded feet. *Fourrure*. It shows its teeth beneath street lanterns and the many eyes may just be discerned in the night air all about floating in their own dimensions. Too much for him, he seeks his way to the striking hexagon, the spiraling six-arrowed star that has lit upon Seville's cathedral to arc its tortuous way across the stone work, some incrudescence of alien machinery or occult circumstance brought upon the city prior to the Inquisition. Who knows what the hexagram holds? The purring beasts of the trees? Perhaps they have something in mind in their arboreal observatories. Summoned to the plaza by the scent of cod. Piscatory picaresque, the roguish creatures prowl the quayside of other towns, moving with humans, buried with humans, enshrined by humans.

Carmona

Carmo Homs Emèse Cybele Attis—gods and temples, localized emissions of the bloody divine under the tutelage of Rome. Many gods but they don't listen to the tedious gibes of mortals. So we say *basta*, holding onto our organs before anyone with a sickle should come along. Attis playing upon the mountainside with his nymph. Where is the fun in that? Blood rites know no time limit, need no gods, no mythology. Excoriate the glans—it's obviously their pleasures that pervert society, turn it upside down we are merely its precursors wary watchers for the moment of riot. The blood of the bull down the sluice sprayed across their backs. The manifestation of a single drop bleeding across an eye to cast its red glare over the world. Eagles nesting on our skulls, the dormant fools lounging on street corners.

8

Eliogabalus before his chariot drawing the black betyl through the crowds.

Italica

Night by night through the stone corridors of the labyrinth inwards and deeper and further beyond the salamander and the sea panther, beyond the centaur and the ephebe, night by night down lanes of unknown cities, meeting Chaldeans who lay out stones upon the counter marked with owls and ants, juxtaposing times and places with assurance. The voice that rises from the darkness to tell mysteries. There are too many paths to recall, too many taken in what must be more than one life. Night by night, we sink into the seas among the radiant spheres of phosphorescent medusae and the shattering camouflage of squid. The friends of youth speak to us about childhood shoes and the leather worn subsequently in these abandoned years. From the forests of spires you work your way through to the faceted buildings with no way in, this is the lengthening maze to initiate in whatever knowledge is to be gotten—I can't pretend to know. The warbling lion's contrary gaze challenges the traveller seeking the fallen star. Even the desert, especially the desert, lives within the labyrinth, the unformed maze with barriers that shift in the wind and chasms opening on all sides. It's the blank shadow of the mosaic eating and being eaten by order, both simultaneously and convulsively in turn. At times you experience great surges forward and make phenomenal discoveries, uncapping the vial of insight and drinking distilled images. Musics arise from the walls beyond the sistra and the xylophone, Dionysus' kettle drums. Snail shell spirals of inward curving chambers take you to peculiar holies of holies long in disuse. Night by night with age and increasing sight you travel across the barrier once blocked by stones and beneath continents following the ship of the sun.

Behind you, the message you've left on the stone.

Cadiz

This pendular distraction, the clock swinging in its dark case above the molten core, the magnetic flux, the pendulum of the poles. The easeful scythe parting the crop in its seething burnish over the plains like a taut, silk curtain drawn up into sky carrying with its folds the shadows of events. My hand falters, loses grip on the handle at the pinnacles of sight, stars tick across the ecliptic. Muzzy headed we disrobe in the tepidarium, laving pates with cool jets of water like

9

streams of marble down the stare of a faun. It excites no penalties, incurs no wrath, to step down the stone stairwell to the thermal springs and veins of gold that circulate beneath our city like some vast mycelium beneath the fungal bloom. It thinks for itself in mineral jets and reflected gleams, the eros of the caverns. Psyche hardly drifts, translated instantly throughout this web—its spider she thrums it carefully, takes in the aeolian throb of the night.

Cueva de la Pileta

Cast shadows like fishing lines into depths and draw forth what forms, what fissures within the mind that open up what vistas? These cracks splitting up the rock face of our stony featured day. In their shadows they may move along abysses of other worlds. Unbalanced, a man holds up his hand and falls; a cheetah smiles from a tree limb overlooking the vast quiet chasm. So long humility and we snap our fingers at the virtues of the age as each crumbles into the porous limestone mass of our synaptic caverns. If we did not have these echoic chambers where would our freedom lie? There's a soft, melancholic undertone to the air here and the shadows cast by the buildings stretch straight to the horizon. Far be it for me to argue for a better way—there are darker ways, freer tracks to move unseen through the subsurface of life.

Tissue wrapping soap bubbles animated and articulated in the most peculiar ways to shamble through its own features those dreams, forgotten millennia ago by people whose languages even are unguessable much less their thoughts but still they thrum in this visionary palace that surges on its spiraling path. Five fingered and waving in silhouette, a hand bidding you *au revoir* from the open canopy of a speedster, some film starlet creating her own image for the limestone screen. The ochre tinted patina of the past. Hades is a human place, a metropolis we built in our finest sandstone. Its traps and snares each have their escapes, but the labyrinth never lets go.

Elvira

Landscape becomes palimpsest in the hands of neolithic farmers at the ard slicing earth beneath oxen feet, carving passage like a vessel pulled by the winds across hardscrabble seas sewn by the comets. There are flints knapped by ancient and bloodied hands in the sods and swells of tumuli, barrows, and the middens that mark our presence. We burrow in the dirt, sharks of the wheat we sow and bury our gods in the hand-coiled pots scorched by raw fire. Time was when people knew where they were by the taste of the air and the salt of their tears spelt out destinies upon glacial sheets in melting letters. I'm here only as an impartial observer, walking among events like a shadow casting blindness behind it. The hard look that cuts into the moment to reveal the magnetized poles of action brings its own field to bear and distorting distorts all with the very hallucinatory capacity that the poles of our eyes illuminate as depth. This field of vision propagates from the eyes, their rotating skein. Streamers catch in trees or windowpanes, cast-off husks of old events that mark the cityscape, their dissolving forms briefly visible in the dodgy optics. At times I only see the relief of your body, a mold of your presence, rays shining like talons from your genitals and hands. The hawks monitor the husks, scattering them with a shriek or a sudden sweep of a wing. At Los Millares we held our own for as long as we could.

Cordoba

Deeper in the forest of pillars sprouting arches that house the depths of further pillared trees on in that reddish gloom of a thousand years there where sigils flow overhead in the forgotten alphabets of forms made by the sky as it cuts through leaves and branches: A signal from the vast cold exterior, the ice-bound sun of the polar coordinates, the north star. Voices echo through this stone expanse and the larval forms of those voices race blindly after them through the air. The sick come here either to be taken or for the vision that will be their cure. They leave a colony behind and duty discharged are free to go, vessel sailing on the etheric winds of glassy form reflecting great streams of plasma and gamma radiation. So slow does it seem to move that the colonists still watch it a century later, their north star.

We didn't last long it must be said before the curious pangs of nature took sway and we followed the track through the forest to a spot we never escaped, never wished to, I suppose. Loaded with the cares of a bitter hive we brought up our battles before the queen, but she'd fled long before.

Albaicín

The word machine that dispenses phrases from shelves with the insertion of a quarter and spools out scrolls of prophecy to the supplicant coin pusher. This is a fine means to lull you into dreamy distraction this business of unscrolling the text to hear the automat's voice. We set sail through the streets past the graffitoed flowers and those blank poles in the darkness behind which certain horror takes place. But we've got the script to rely upon, our periplous for the stone maze, and everywhere we turn the signals tells us of presences unseen in the air and the vengeance those below would take on them.

And yet we've no need to wind ourselves into a cul-de-sac—the routes abound in tunnels, flooded passages, skyways, and sea roads. A black cat marks out his own riverside path through the grass beneath crumbling ramparts and ruins of empires bestrode with fig trees, lianas, ice cream vendors. Here the castle broods over the hills, no one to be seen in its towers, its form reflected in the clouds above where comedies played out by simulacra amuse the watching drones. But the shock of it all is simple—an iron bell clanging through the bastions and echoing down every corridor in its tooth-shattering wall of sound, the sonics of state terror. The memory of rifle shots, lines of distant figures disappearing. How is it to be then cease to exist in an instant without any warning—no you left to be stopped, where does the momentum of subjectivity move to? The rocks and the cicadas that have seen more than they wish? What happens then at that instantaneous death by sniper shot?

Ataraxia

Mind forms the void, a signal, comfort in this chaos and finds announcements of a curious rigor drawing out the reins of the future to pull forward into that zone, that unseen plain beyond the mountain's crest where a sun lurks hidden. And these discoveries curl inward upon themselves in their own eras, take on character and inform personality, corralling into a tourbillon of energetic thought that eventually snuffs itself from the moment. Where those flung to borderlands make their way is no one's business but their own. Yet trailing through the history of these winnowed thoughts and whirlpools of words and images cast along like flotsam dissipating, coalescing, the filmy gauze flickers cloud to cloud to land on a distracted gaze. Lords that have no mercy, the vocabularies of rustic times deploy themselves in new ranks, mooning their adversaries. Punishment is meted out and the spoils divided before rapine, a word hoard plundered and plundered again, that old word "whore" always at the lips.

Alhambra

Where do they halt in their path across the plaza? Where do they find water on the stone plain? The detritus of the invading army left in the wagon ruts and scattered about in a waste of land that even these soldiers don't see fit to conquer. What terrible threat speaks out of these cliffs when the wind strokes the limestone edges like a bow? We test the air for toxic flies that spiral unseen in the night before daring to take the road again, our jar returning from its plunge in the dark with a light boring sound and the chime of a crystal bell. Here you find it uneasy to proceed in any direction but inward, and that it turns out is all too deep an abyss to force through in your trajectory. The lurking hint of a traumatic scene hampers the approach to the doorway. Mother and father closeted in the linen cabinet only an eyeball visible among the layers of sheets. Fine, move on through the pre-arranged ruins to take away from them what keepsakes you may—Volubilis to Italica the army marched the limits. If a legionnaire harasses on the road learn your Latin quickly but move on. The wizened flesh of the landscape, the tortuous skin of a desert oak picked apart by the glassy sands, the trash piles capped by human heads that look on quizzically, sphinxlike in their need to draw from travelers the certainty of the final word. It's a day for the elderberry bush that heals in its purplish ichor. The soldier hoards a branch in a leather pouch about his neck believing its mere presence will stave off plague. They perform speedy decapitations by the roadside, mark their path with crucifixions and the massacre of the unwelcoming. Furor takes them as a god would and leaves nothing behind.

The starry castle on the hillside, however, stands untouched, marking the errors from its sixteen windows and the hours from the advance of their sunlit holes. Out of this artificial cave the world is projected in its radiant spectacle across the fields of destruction, glyphs that cleave their paths.

2

HOY Y NO ABAJO
Verónica Cabanillas Samaniego

Comprendo mi ira
Fugaz relámpago
Arma letal puesta en tu frente
Y disparo tantas veces como quiera
Como necesitan las angustias
Salir a incendiar lo que adentro calcina
Con el polvo del conocimiento
Ese que hacia ustedes pulveriza
Y a mí me deja un hueco
Hondo
Donde persigo mi luz
Esa que estalla a la velocidad indemne en que vuela esto innombrable
Parecido a la barbaridad
Tan violento puede ser decir algo certero que se parezca a la verdad
Tan violento puede ser estar unos pasos más allá
Abajo
Sépanlo
Donde la ira se fermenta
Y es la respuesta ante el horror y el insulto
Los lenguajes se desintegran
El estado disociado
Lo sagrado una vez tocado
El resto
La realidad
Los hombres de negro que persiguen
Todo entra de golpe
Hacia el fondo
Como una masa derramada
En una imagen delirante
Estar en sí mismo
Ni el verbo ser entiende
Cómo se hace carne el delirio
Pero quien razona allí
Sabe de los enemigos reales
Y atenta
Porque es lo único que importa
Hasta dar la vida misma
Para salvar la vida

Porque es necesario inventarnos una nueva vida
Y si no se empieza a gritar, a atentar, a destruir cada institución
Hasta la disociación del cuerpo, ese cosificado, institución numeral
Hasta híper fragmentar la realidad
Con esos ojos que vieron el estallido, la luz partida en mil moviendo las cosas
Aferrándote al delirio, porque aquí no hay más que muerte
Y la cabeza explota
A esos extremos lleva la lucidez y la fineza del amor
Aproximaciones le llaman
¿A qué?
¿Hacia dónde?
Y ¿por qué uno no otro?
Aprendí a ver el destino
A descifrar los sueños
A llegar a altamar
¡Oh! ¡Raza de seres humanos!
En ti me vi Leonora
Como una pequeña con su cuento de Alicia
Repartiéndolo
Y. . . ¿qué me diste?
Nada
Esas cosas no tienen precio
Leonora lo supo, y pintó y escribió como la única
Porque las luchas genuinas
Que arrasan las ciudades y los cuerpos interiores
Que traspasan las fronteras
La verdadera batalla
Se da dentro
Y no hay que esperar ningún premio
Es por ello esa calidad de altura moral
¿Se entiende?
Abajo no es un libro
Va caminando
Como un ciego entre ciegos
Preguntando
¿Qué es la locura?
Hallaste muchas respuestas y encontraste la vida y el esplendor
Más allá de los muros y las sogas que te ataban
Siempre supiste de tu gloria
Pero *Abajo* sigue aquí con nosotros
Y no saben ni lo más mínimo para interpretar
Dicen. . . esas palabras
Porque *Abajo* no es un libro
Ni un testimonio
No está hecho de palabras
Es donde pasan algunos

15

Donde rozan el desgarro y entran
Valientes
Para saber que estar abajo es tan humano
Tan natural
Tan necesario
Una experiencia que debería ser el pan
En estos tiempos de crisis
Un pan por probar que nos confronte
Así quizá, algún día la surrealidad entre, brote y se instaure
Y no exista ese libro
Nada más que como evidencia del error.
Leonora te veo en la sala de hospital
Viajando a Santander
En una camilla rodeada de enfermeras que quieren disuadirte de esos
pensamientos peligrosos
Porque el psiquiatra va a llegar y quizá persigue a su madre y a la religión
Olvidaste a tu padre
El mío miraba
Y yo creo ser tú
Sólo para sentir tu inmensa soledad en semejanza a la mía
El jardín y Egipto o el fin del mundo en la tv
El asesino de turno a quien acabar
Imagino tus ojos dando vueltas
Girando
Separados de los míos
Ese estado que tanto asusta a la convención de los burgueses
Creyendo cambiar el rumbo de la humanidad;
Moviendo los dedos
O las ramitas de los arboles
O quemando los naipes sobre el velador
Moviendo el universo al apagar la luz
Creyendo que Jerusalén y el paraíso entero está en el jardín de tu
psiquiátrico
Leonora,
Me he recostado en ti
Hoy
Y no abajo
Aquí, desde donde puedo
Venida de lejos como tú
Hacer algo por la vida
La enfermedad abre senderos
Para poder ver
Para saber ver
Para poder hacer;
La obra
Esa otredad maravillosa que se instaurará
Sigamos moviendo los hitos

Milímetro a milímetro
Un poco más allá
Esa es la distancia que te parece incalculable
que te produce pavor
¡Oh! ¡Humanidad!.

(A Leonora... aunque mi deliro extraña al tuyo, y en la distancia su eco sobre
el desierto me dio esa calma que buscaba)

3

Doctor Guilder's Asylum
Alan Gullette

The Seraphim Health Center occupies a large brownstone building at
the corner of Westchester and Hayes. Above the entrance there is a
plaque with the carved image of a winged serpent.

Dr. Rudolph Guilder was the institute's founder and had gained
recognition for his work with delusional schizophrenics. The subject
interested me as a writer, because writers are always in search of
interesting characters to portray in their stories, characters in crisis –
for it's under extreme stress that the components of the personality
start to unravel and reveal themselves. And what better place to
study characters in crisis than in a madhouse?

"Dr. Guilder will see you now," said the nurse. She had a stern look
that challenged me to make her smile by saying something funny.

"In that case, I will see Dr. Guilder now," I said.

It was more silly than funny, and instead of smiling she looked
puzzled and noted my grin mechanically before she led me into the
office.

The doctor sat behind his desk, looking out the window with his back toward me.

The nurse placed a folder on his desk and left, closing the door.

The room had a Victorian feel and lots of nice dark wood: wainscot panels, elaborate framing around windows and doorways – even the ceiling was decorated with molding.

"Hello?" The doctor said, still facing the other way.

"Hello?" I replied, assuming he was speaking to me. He swiveled around and saw me standing there, and for the first time I saw that he was on the phone.

"Have a seat," he said to me in a lowered voice, holding the receiver away from his mouth.

The doctor was balding and wore a beard, otherwise there was no resemblance to Freud. He wore a linen jacket, Henley shirt and blue jeans. I wasn't sure if Guilder was a German name, but I half-expected the psychiatrist to have a German accent, as was the stereotype in psychiatry... However, Dr. Guilder spoke perfect American English with a mid-western accent.

"Yes, yes," he said as I was sitting.

"No, in Fregoli delusion the patient believes various people he meets are really the same person in disguise. Capgras delusion is the one where the patient believes that a relative or spouse has been replaced by an impostor... Right."

The phone call ended and the doctor give me his undivided attention.

"As I mentioned in my letter, I'm a writer – you may be familiar with my surrealist poetry – or my weird fiction? No? Anyway... now I'm working on a book about people with delusions, and as soon as I began my research I learned about you and your work here. That's why I wrote: I wanted to visit in person to find out more about the various disorders and how they are treated."

The doctor watched me carefully as I spoke, then glanced at a paper on his desk.

"Well, I don't know what you've heard or read so far, but in general a delusional disorder is a serious mental illness. The deluded person cannot tell the difference between what is real and what is imagined – that's the hallmark of psychosis."

He was sitting up so straight that I became self-conscious of my posture, which tends to be poor. It seemed that I was slumping, so I sat up straight too.

"In the past, society did not know how to respond to mental illness. It was believed that the individual was possessed by a demon and therefore feared, locked away, even killed. At best, they have been misunderstood and disregarded, an exception to the rule of normality. But of course, more recently the need to address the problem as its own phenomenon has been perceived and so psychology and psychiatry have developed."

"But they're still viewed as abnormal, ill," I inserted.

"Yes... perhaps an even more enlightened view would be that they are gifted in some way and therefore have something to offer society. In a different culture they might be guided to become shamans or seers – visionaries – even artists, writers and poets." He smiled on the last word.

"What types of delusions are we talking about?" I asked.

"Each one is different, each case unique, though they typically fall into certain categories. But they all involve a false belief that persists in the face of evidence or rational argument. Most often, but not always, the belief involves a mundane situation that could be true, but isn't true in this case. For example, I might think I'm the King of Spain – which is possible, but not true. In a few cases, the person will believe something bizarre, impossible, like they were born on the moon."

"Give it time..." I said under my breath.

"What's that?" he asked, not quite hearing.

"Oh, nothing. Please go on."

"Sometimes it takes time to develop, sometimes it happens all at once. Unfortunately, people with delusions commonly lack insight into themselves and often don't know they have a problem, so they don't seek help and their condition deteriorates to the point they need hospitalization. If they do recognize that they have a problem, they're often too embarrassed to seek help – or afraid of doctors, or afraid to find out... and again, things get worse."

"Would it be possible to meet some of the patients – I mean, assuming they are not violent or dangerous!"

"Well, our patients are fairly harmless. The kind of violent case you are referring to is a matter for the county hospital... Yes, well, I have a busy schedule this afternoon, but I can introduce you to some of the male patients on the second floor – they're segregated by gender, you see."

As we stood up he said, "Perhaps it would be best if you leave your notebook here for the time being. It might make the patients nervous or more reluctant to talk."

"Oh, sure," I agreed. "Fortunately, I have excellent memory."

1. At the Spa

The doctor led me out of his office, past the nurse's desk, and across the waiting area to the stairs. The whole place had a homey feeling that extended to carpet on the stairs. I followed him up past the first floor to the second, where an orderly sat beside a small table in the hallway. He stood up without a word and the doctor introduced us.

"Mr. Gullette, this is Arnold, our orderly on this floor; Mr. Gullette is writing a book about delusions."

Arnold showed little emotion but eyed me suspiciously.

"I'll take you in to see the first patient, then Arnold will introduce you to the others. Later we can meet to compare notes – so to speak!"

Arnold rapped twice on the door to Room 1 before opening it outward and stepping aside. The doctor led me in.

"This is, uh, Mr. Reginald Periwinkle," said the doctor, introducing me to the patient. He smiled when he said the name.

"How do you do," said the patient politely, with a nod or slight bow.

There was an air of nobility about him – of refinement, cultured breeding. He had a full beard and pointy mustache, silver hair, doming brow, rosy complexion. He spoke with a deep, warm voice, somewhat theatrical, and tended to use a declamatory tone.

The doctor left but Arnold remained at the open door, leaning against the frame and looking now into the room, now down the hall.

There were two chairs and Mr. Periwinkle offered me one, so I sat in one and he sat in the other.

"So, how long have you been here?" I asked to begin with.

"Such a difficult question to answer, like a math puzzle... How can you count the days when none of the days seem like days, and the nights don't seem like nights?

"At first I could tell time by the meals – the service was regular! The meals came in sets: breakfast, lunch, tea, and dinner. But they served us six or seven sets of meals every twelve hours – and you expect me to keep track of the days? Now time leaves no shape in my memory, the days just come and go, like the oil of Bergamot..."

"How did you come to be here?" I asked, trying another tack.

"My reservation was made under an assumed name, Mr. Periwinkle (wink, wink!). Travelling incognito to terra incognita. No one knows and no one asks!

My real title is 3rd Earl of Sussex and I am Her Majesty's Exchequer." He puffed up his chest with the last part, then lowered his voice as if to speak confidentially.

"I normally don't divulge my true identity, but I can see you are a discriminating, intelligent person, trustworthy, and well-educated."

"Well, it so happens that you were in the paper today – the Exchequer, that is," I said, remembering an account I had read that morning.

"Oh?" he reacted suspiciously. "What have they said about me now?"

"I didn't read the whole article, something about the European Union... Funny thing is, it said that you were in Brussels today..." I decided to press him a little on his belief.

"Of course I am!" he said, matter-of-factly. "How do you think I keep up with matters!" "Then you are there now?"

"Sir, we are there. That's undeniable."

"But there's a meeting going on today, this afternoon – now. You are here with me, but the Exchequer is in the meeting with the Europeans."

"Aha! It's that impostor again! As soon as I turn my back, he's at it, impersonating me at all the official affairs..."

"That must explain it," I said, not wanting to threaten his delusion any further. "May I ask why you are here – at Dr. Guilder's?"

"My personal physician suggested this Spa, time to kick back, so to speak. And no one knows – mind you! Shhh! That's part of the rest, you see, or everyone would be clamoring... Especially after that trying affair in Prescott Place..."

"What happened in Prescott Place"

He rolled his eyes. "Do you really want to go into that again?"

I wondered what he meant, since we hadn't gone into it before. "Only if you want to," I suggested.

"It's the same as always," he said, getting frustrated if not angry. "The incivility of the servants, the instability of their servitude, the insurrection of the peasantry – it all comes to the same! In brief, they don't do what you tell them to do!" He said loudly, with big eyes bulging, full of righteous indignation. Then he quieted down.

"I know it's not right to get angry – upset. Have to watch my blood pressure..." He was silent for a full minute.

"When I reflect upon the matter in calm fashion, I suppose I can see why they perform their duties in so begrudging a manner – after all, each of them would rather be in my shoes – patent leather, shiny buckles! So they could tread on me – 'Don't tread on me!'" He shouted, and Arnold leaned into the door frame to see what was happening.

"So, we have problems, but who doesn't? Problems in the past, due to the failure of others to recognize my authority... Problems in the present due to my absence, but we can't be bothered with details! We are the Exchequer!

"The rents, the taxes, utilities and groceries – do you expect me to sign every check and tally?

"What's the exchange rate? Ask the Exchequer!" Then be began singing:

> Pennies for penses,
> pence for sense,
> 100 pfennigs leave
> a mark in the dark...

After one verse he stopped himself and looked over at Arnold, still standing in the doorway with a constant look of disapproval.

"When did you realize you that were, uh, Lord Sussex?"

"Oh, that's a silly question! You can't trick me with that... By the way, Lord Rathmore is coming next week. Owing largely, I think, to my own recommendation. It helps one gather one's thoughts. But commoners can be so boring!

"What about your family history?"

"You'll have to go pretty far back to find where my family tree began... It's on a hill in Salisbury! Be sure to take a clean cloth – to wipe the dust from the coat of arms... Caught on the coast by armies of the night...

"Vagabonds and heathens, too, trying to muck up the heirlooms, when we had dug them out of the peat bog!"

Then he had a hearty laugh, as to a private joke. "Carry a torch back with you. Dark by night, dark by day. That's why I left!" And he laughed again – broke into a fit of laughter, broken only by coughing.

Arnold stepped into the room. "Dr. Guilder wants me to take you to the next patient now."

And so I waved goodbye to "Mr. Periwinkle" (still chuckling) and followed Arnold across the hall to Room 2.

2. I've Got a Secret

"This is Gary Tuttle," said Arnold as I went into the room. He assumed his usual post hovering at the open door.

The patient was a young man – early to mid-twenties – and seemed to smile without a reason. Glassy eyes shone wide as he rolled his head back slightly to acknowledge your presence. A perpetual, knowing smile, like he knows something that you don't know – and he can tell you are aware of this fact... You know the game.

As soon as I sat in the guest chair, Mr. Tuttle took a look at Arnold, who was looking down the hall and seemed to be out of earshot, and began to whisper. "The CIA is running this place. It's all a front to get me to tell my secrets."

"What secrets?" I asked.

"Nice try!" he said with his knowing smile.

"How do you know it's the CIA and not the FBI?" I asked.

He thought about it and smiled. "Because we're not in America anymore, bucko!"

"Oh? Where are we then?"

"Why, that's a secret!"

"Ha ha... uh, I get it," and soon I was matching his giddy smile with one of my own. "You see, I've made an important discovery that I have to reveal to someone – but not to just anyone. No, only to the President, or the UN chief, or someone like that. That's how important it is." He seemed sincere.

"May I ask when did you discovered this... secret?"

"When I was ten years old, I realized I was a secret agent."

"You were a secret agent?" I repeated.

"Yes."

"When you were ten years old?"

"That's right. Still am."

"And how did that come about?"

He thought about it for a moment. "I've been talking with Dr. Guilder about it... As I understand it, there was a kind of awakening of self-consciousness. That's how he put it. I became aware of the limitation of others' awareness – which meant, the privacy of my own mind... Does that make sense?" He seemed uncertain himself, wanted reinforcement.

"Uh, yeah, kinda."

"But I had to keep it secret from others."

"A secret – that you knew..."

"And even if they knew, I couldn't let on that I knew that they knew – you see? Otherwise I'd only confirm their suspicion that I was a secret agent. Then it wouldn't be secret anymore!" And he laughed. "You know the game." Again the knowing smile, the giddy tilt of the head... Something wasn't clear.

"Who are you a secret agent for?" I asked.

He looked at me incredulously.

"I can't tell you that! That's something nobody knows. But it's part of what I have to convey."

"Your secret message?"

"Right. You have to protect yourself," he said, giving serious advice. "When you're walking, the faces of the other pedestrians seem to convey a message – telling you to look out, someone ahead is dangerous or not to be trusted – things like that."

As he spoke his eyes flitted about the room, as if he imagined he was on a busy sidewalk and he was looking from person to person, up and down.

"Even the way a person walks can be a sign about something, so I have to try to read it, understand the signal... Everyone looks at you, but how much do they really know? Can I trust them with my secret? Do they have a secret to tell me?"

His eyes fixed on a point in the room and I turned to look. There was nothing there.

"When a stranger looks at you, it's as if he knows your inmost soul. So you have to be careful. I have to hold on to it, don't you see? It's the most fundamental thing."

"How long have you been here?" I asked, but he didn't answer. His smile turned to a frown.

"This whole place is a front!" he said, then quieted down and spoke in a whisper. "The doctor, the orderlies, the nurses, all of the patients – it's all a sham. They're just paid actors! I wonder how much they get..." His voice returned to normal volume and his face returned to a smile.

"They all leave at night, but I can't leave. They lock me in, keep me tight – tick tock, the game is locked, nobody else can play!

"They used to give me passes."

"Passes?"

"But they don't let me out anymore, never again. It's too much trouble to run around and set things up."

"Set things up?" I repeated.

"Yeah, you know, all the facades..." And he laughed. "I used to drive on the freeway just to make them work! Whenever I got close to seeing them set up the scenery, the traffic got thick and slowed me down. They've got everyone in on it! Not sure about you, though... You seem okay."

Arnold, who had disappeared for a while, reappeared at the open door and the patient fell silent.

"Okay, Mr. Gullette, we're ready for you to see the next patient." As we left and Arnold closed the door, I caught a final glimpse of Mr. Tuttle's face. The look changed as dramatically as if a mask had fallen away – from joy to resignation, from a mad smile to a look of mild horror.

3. I am the World and the World is Me!

"This is Scott Milner," said Arnold, introducing me to the next patient. "Scott, this is Alan."

"Hi, Alan. I am the World and the World is Me!" he said.

"How's that?" I asked, as if I hadn't heard.

"I am the World and the World is Me!" He repeated his slogan proudly. "Dr. Guilder said my body is coterminous with the earth. He called me geosomatic – and I may be the first!"

"Interesting," I said, having never heard of such a thing. "How did this 'coterminous' relationship come about?"

"It happened when I was a teenager and I got my first pimple. When it popped, Mount St. Helens erupted. That was no coincidence!"

"That was it?"

"That's when I knew I had a special connection to things. When I cried, it rained. When I danced, the leaves danced. When I stretched my spine, the mountains rippled, causing earthquakes and avalanches.

"For a while I was afraid to move at all, afraid I'd cause a catastrophe somewhere. I just remained still for a long time – I mean for a couple days...

"During that time I had to really concentrate. You don't know how hard it is to make the cactus bloom.

"Then I began to hear voices."

"Voices?"

"Yeah, voices in different parts of my body."

"Your body parts speak to you? What do they say?"

"You know... they tell me when to move, so it would be okay. Like the voice in my foot would say 'Ok to move' and the voice in my ankle would echo it, and so on up the leg, then I could take a step in safety. No Calabrian landslides. No earthquakes in North Cambria. No monsoons in Calcutta."

He chuckled. "Fortunately, my stomach said 'ok to laugh' – or you never know what might happen! "Now you understand how I am the World. Conversely and consequently, the reverse is also true: The

26

World is Me. The breeze makes me happy; when I'm happy, there's a breeze. It doesn't matter which comes first, because – 'I am the World and the World is Me!'"

It was becoming a familiar refrain.

"That is, I feel the effects of the earth movements and the raging seas... I hear violent noises in my head like gunshots: war somewhere, or a lightning storm... Of course, things have gotten better with the anti-psychotic drugs, but still, from time to time, I have an episode – you know, 'Earth to Scott.' And sometimes it's just too much. My gravity is lost. 'The center cannot hold...' It's overwhelming! Everything flies away from me, like an explosion has gone off inside. The connection between things is lost... The skin is the last chance to hold things together – the crust of the earth – or everything would fall apart – the earth would explode and fly away into space... Only the skin holds me in and saves the world... Because..." – and he paused for me to join him on the refrain – "'I am the World and the World is Me!'" Said in unison.

At that point, Arnold appeared and signaled it was time to move on.

"Wait, let me show you the Rock of Gibraltar!" Mr. Milner called behind me, but Arnold closed his door.

4. The Key Agents of History

"This is Professor Bain," Arnold said, introducing me to the patient in Room 4. I went in, but Prof. Bain was preoccupied and didn't notice me at first. With Wayfarer glasses, graying temples, pipe in mouth, and wearing a tweed jacket with elbow patches, he certainly looked the part.

He sat at his desk, hard at work on something. The desk was crowded with stacks of books, notepads, and loose sheets of paper. When he finally noticed me, he looked at me with concern before registering my presence in his mind. Setting down his pipe (which wasn't lit), he stood up abruptly, as if following a strict sense of politeness and decorum.

"Ah! I'm Professor Bain, and you must be Walter." He extended his hand. "I've been expecting you."

I took his hand automatically while thinking of what to say. "But I'm not Walter."

"Not Walter?"

"No, my name is Alan."

He was confused, a bit distressed, and turned to his desk to look for a piece of paper. "I'm sure they said your name would be Walter..." but he failed to find it. He took a piece paper, wadded it up, and tossed it against the wall. "I have to burn these letters in the fireplace," he said, looking at the wall next to my chair. I looked too. Of course, there was no fireplace in a place like this, only a pile of paper wads.

"It's no good to leave documents like that lying around... Nevertheless, I'm glad you finally showed up!"

"Showed up?"

"Yes, you don't know how long I've been asking for a Graduate Assistant to help me with my work!"

He was so happy that I didn't want to let him down, but neither did I want to lead him on. "I see, but I'm not..." I tried to object, but he cut me off.

"That's alright, I'm sure your qualifications are up to par. I can tell right away that you're a bright student."

It was awkward, but I went along.

"I was beginning to think you wouldn't come at all... The Faculty Senate is trying to force me out – but I have tenure! All because of my ideas – my 'wild ideas.' Tell, me, when was there ever an important new theory that wasn't first pooh-poohed? Par for the course."

"And what is your theory, Professor?"

"I thought you'd never ask! How you ever heard of the Giboras?"

"Uh, no, I can't say that I have."

"I'm not surprised – it's the best kept secret in history! But it turns out they were involved in everything, the key Agents of History that no one has ever heard of – behind every important historical event in the books."

"Really?"

"And my work bears it out..." "The Giboras, you say?"

"Part syndicate, part family, part secret brotherhood... the Key Figures were everywhere... at Key Points: Ying Zheng, Genghis Khan, Marco Polo, Garibaldi... William Burbage, Jethro Tull, Marconi, Leibniz... The names are not random – as numerology reveals."

He put his left hand on a stack of papers at the corner of the desk.

"Not to mention Leonardo," he added, and he seemed to bask in the warm inner glow that resonated from the name.

"The Angel of the Mons was not a play on a stage... Romulus wasn't Roman, you see!" "Who were they and where did they come from?" I asked.

"That's the question! I'm glad you're with me." He got excited and jumped up, then began to pace back and forth in the small room. "Oh boy, this will be great! There's the course, the book, maybe even a documentary film... We have to do it all at once, no time to waste! I was just talking to a publisher who wants to bring out the book." He paused and scrutinized my face closely, perhaps looking for clues of remembrance, then continued. "The firm wants to bring out a variorum edition, hardback of course – with a paperback to follow, in due time – though it will be in the spring, assuming the hardback comes out in the fall. They have a whole promotional campaign planned... Anyway, they will have an introduction by the eminent Dr. Jenkins, who apparently has taken a fancy to my theory..."

He allowed himself to feel both vindicated and proud.

"But the point is, the book with have everything... We'll have an index that cross- references all of the important figures – and a chart – I've been working on a chart showing the interrelations of the prime movers – not a hierarchy but a historical family tree of sorts, showing descents and declinations of various lines of thought-action brought about by the Agents throughout recorded history..."

He paused, out of breath, and caught it, then turned to take a drink of water from the glass on his podium. He looked tired, even haggard.

"You look tired, professor."

"I never sleep – don't need sleep – no more than three hours and I'm full of energy. Working on the book is incredibly important! Sometimes I may go for days without sleep, but I don't feel tired. The work creates its own energy!"

His voice rose to the level of a shout, drawing the attention of Arnold, who stepped into the room and told the professor to calm down.

Prof. Bain apologized. "Well, I see you have another class to go to... We will discuss this further tomorrow..." And I left.

5. Love's Lover

"This is David Singer," said Arnold.

You could tell that the patient had been lying down: there were sheet marks on his face. We shook hands but his hand was limp, lifeless.

He had dark circles around his eyes; his eyes were dim, the gaze far away. He seemed depressed like someone in grief. Had he been crying?

"I saw her only once – a single glimpse – but that was enough." When he spoke, his voice rang with a mournful tone. Melancholy was painted on his face.

"I chanced to glance across the room and through the window, across the street. With parasol and flowers in her hand, standing in the moving crowd; she seemed to look at me. With emerald eyes and freckled cheeks – and her figure was complete... All fairy tales and myth aside, she truly was 'the fairest of the fair.' "Neither high born, nor low born, she was pure born. She was my Helen, my Guinevere, my Cleopatra and my Beatrice." Already speaking poetic speech, he added a refrain:

wine, rose, vine
and the vines grow together

"I pursued anyone who looked like my Beatrice. I thought I saw her again: in a fish market, in a diamond market; at the library book sale, at the opera. I pursued her around the world, trying to capture her – but how can you capture a wild Giselle, a butterfly, a will o' the wisp, the very spirit of freedom?

I was in love – but where was my lover?

"I was in love – but who did I love?

"Was I in love with Love itself?

"And Love performs an Alchemy: Love transforms the eyes, and the eyes see a world transformed, transfused with beams of light fallen from heaven's height.

vine, rose, weeds
and the briars form a thicket

"The sinuous lines of the hills became her curves. Limbs of trees were her limbs. The clouds were the clouds in her eyes. The world had become her body!

"Will she ever come back?

"When she returns she will be as always: like never, like the river, like the summer.

"She was like the carved moment, the fallen martyr, the father mother, patterned matter. "Her solar-eyed song was a subdominant seventh that clings to the web of chords, to the web of stones – like perfume of clouds, like stones of carved moments sought until found – sought in her absence – found in her return.

lime, root, seed
and the seed grows in shadow

"I see the sky through the buildings. Through the sky I see the hills beyond time. "The shadows of comets fall like dust. When the lover dies, she becomes the world... "Now eyelashes bar the windows of my cell

life, love, need
and the heart hides in sadness."

At this point, Arnold came and saved me from the gloom of sorrow that overflowed the patient and filled the room.

My throat ached, like an apricot was caught and I couldn't swallow. My eyes burned, but I didn't cry.

I could see through the barred window at the end of the hall the broken chalice of the sky.

6. I am God and How I Got There

"This is Bob Crabtree," said Arnold, introducing me to the sixth patient.

"Come in, my son," the patient said when he saw me. Tall, long-faced, somewhat gaunt, he spoke with a booming voice.

Did he think he was my father? Or maybe it was a manner of speech. He took my arm and ushered me to a chair, but he remained standing. "Allow me to introduce myself. I am God."

"You mean the God?"

"Yes, God Almighty, Maker of Heaven and Earth!" He beamed proudly.

"I see," I said, impressed by the force of his conviction. I had heard of delusions of grandeur, but this was the grandest of them all!

"Do you mind if I ask you a few questions?"

"Ask and it shall be given…"

"First, how did you come to realize that you are God?"

"I achieved godhead through an arduous Journey, including a Pact with the Devil – a treaty of sorts… But if you ask how: I pierced the space between thoughts, between thinking and perceiving, between things in the world, that tiny sliver between atoms and dimensions, between the sorry starry nights and the summer things we say. And now I am locked up, persecuted, because I told the truth! 'Mine is the suffering, the sorrow and the pity.'"

"If you are God and God is omnipotent, why don't you leave this place?" I asked an obvious question.

"It's all part of the Pact."

"What do you mean by the Pact?"

"Let me explain. First there is the Trial. Conscience is both Judge and Jury. No prosecutor is needed. You are your own prosecutor. The trial is your life. Thus was I brought before my Conscience as before a Judge of the Inquisition. There was a parade of witnesses – victims of my neglect, my lack of concern, like a crying child I once passed on the sidewalk, or a beggar that I ignored.

"Guilt made me guilty! And innocence was lost. I knew my own fate. But I was Judge, too. So I pleaded with myself. Then I saw the truth of human existence, and the vision absolved me."

Heretofore, he had seemed to address the room with his answers. Now he came up close and faced me as he spoke.

"This is the critical point, my friend. Paranoia is conquered when judger and judged are one. All are redeemed in light of Life."

Then he resumed his address to the room.

"But the Pact – my Pact – all the souls in hell, boiling like frogs… Over fires of Remorse, with the fuel of Regret… And all the while, wearing his white mask, Conscience is Satan's right hand man – with whips, cat o' nine tails, and nine lives...

"I was born into fleets of floating iron, bobbing in the Gulf Stream... Forceps plucked me from the waves – light like children laughing – and biceps put me in a lifeboat all my own and shoved me off, free among the reeds, like straws (that's how the mud breathes: air gets sucked down into the mud through reeds)...

"Frogs grogging and gorging... Do you know what it's like to eat flies? To sit in stagnant pond scum on stringy yogi legs and bathe in your own waste? Do you?

"That was the punishment, but what was my crime? To be born! That's the Grand Assumption."

"The Grand Assumption?" I asked, curious about the unusual term.

"Thus was my sentence was handed down," he said in answer. "I had to take up the burden of the world, even though my spine was cracking under the strain of holding up my own gigantic head – this elephantine head – which, as you notice, is bigger than the world that Atlas had to hold on his shoulders.

"And bearing that, to walk on broken glass till your soles are shredded, then on burning coals that sear the flesh and cauterize the wounds. But these wounds will never heal!"

He held up his hands, which appeared to be fine. Again he came face to face, now with a desperate look of horror in his eyes. It's a tremendous burden to bear!" And immediately he added: "But I have helpers, a legion of winged creatures to bear me up and keep me up. All part of the Pact. For mine is the suffering, the sorrow and the pity." He repeated. "Do you suffer in his cage?" I asked, indicating the tiny cell in which he lived.

"No, my suffering is elsewhere. Suffering is my cross to bear. Suffering is my crown of thorns. Not my suffering but the suffering of others: to feel vicariously the pain and psychological turmoil of others – all others.

"I was cursed with the empathy of Christ, endless, bottomless; and like Prometheus and his liver, my organ of conscience grew back each time it was eaten away by the great pecking beaks of Piety and Pity."

"But doesn't being here keep you from your work?"

"On the contrary, I feel everything, observe everything from here just as I would from anywhere. These walls are just an illusion, my friend." He thought about it some more. "I can be God from anywhere; but the terrible burden remains." Thus he divulged his human secret.

7. Deranged

"This is Jason Morgan," said the orderly, introducing me to the patient in Room 7. When I went in, the patient had his back to me. He was busy at his dresser. "Jason?" Arnold called his name louder.

The patient turned.

"This is Mr. Gullette," Arnold explained. "He wants to talk to you now." Jason was in his twenties, like several of the patients I had met. Thin, wiry, stiff, with a constant look of dread.

I extended my hand and he took it automatically, then laughed. "What's funny?" I asked, wondering if he was laughing at me. "I don't shake hands – the hand offers itself…"

And he laughed again.

"When I talk, someone else is shaping the lips and moving the tongue."

Then he looked distracted, as if remembering something, or listening to something I couldn't hear.

"Is it time? Have to check…"

And he returned to the dresser where I had first seen him. Now I could see the objects on the dresser, organized a certain way: a comb; a letter-sized postmarked envelope; a pen; a framed photograph; a stack of coins (though why he'd need them here was a mystery); and a medallion on a chain. His hands moved quickly from object to object, touching and adjusting its position slightly, then revisited them again and again, spending particular attention to shifting the links of the chain.

After going over things three times, he turned back to face me. His eyes studied my face quickly, then looked at the space on either side of me. Then he looked at Arnold in the doorway. Arnold hovered at the door, one moment there and the next gone. Then he disappeared for a long time, and each time I looked for him he wasn't there. It was unnerving, like the feeling of being watched when no one is there.

"Look at the mirror," Jason said.

I turned to see that he was facing a mirror that hung on the wall near the dresser.

"That guy seems familiar," he said, pointing at the mirror, "but I can't find him in the room – you see? It's a trick mirror – another trick by Dr. Guilder! You can't see vampires in a mirror. Who is that guy? I can't quite place him."

He was referring to his own reflection.

"Is it time? Have to check..." And again he was at the dresser, making sure everything was there and in its proper place. Three times over. Then he turned and seemed to be listening again – straining to hear something out of earshot.

"Do you hear something?" I finally asked.

"Yes, I hear voices."

"What do the voices say?"

"Right now... I can't tell you. But sometimes they tell me not to eat, or sleep, or that I have to keep walking on and on and on. But I can't walk here."

"When do you hear them?"

"Oh, all the time – they're all around me, in the sound of the wind, the rustle of trees, the sound of footsteps."

I strained to hear whatever he might be hearing. At one point I did hear voices, then realized the sound came from down the hall, where the nurse and doctor were speaking in low tones.

"There's a constant story going on," he continued. "The words circle like a flock of birds before they decide to land."

"What's the story about?"

"It's about my life, the whole history of past deeds... It just goes on." And he laughed again, as if at a private joke. "It's hard to talk to you, because I'm not sure if I'm really talking and if it's you that's talking back."

From where I sat, I could see through the open door and across the hall into Room 8. It looked empty and the bed seemed freshly made – and inviting. The nonstop series of patient visits had been an ordeal, and it would be nice to take a rest.

Meanwhile, Jason went on as if I wasn't there, addressing the room, talking to no one, staring at particulars.

"Is it time? I have to check. Seconds ticking, gotta keep track."

This time, instead of going to the dresser, he simply froze where he stood in the middle of the room. He was completely still, catatonic, staring into space.

When Arnold finally returned, I realized that I, too, had been sitting motionless for some time, simply watching the patient's behavior. Beside Arnold stood the nurse, also observing me with a look of concern.

8. What's Normal?

As I suspected, Room 8 was unoccupied – and empty apart from a bed and a chair. But I was surprised to see the doctor sitting on the chair, awaiting my arrival. It was generous of him to make time after the long afternoon to talk to me.

Since there was nowhere else to sit, I sat on the bed. It seemed awkward to sit on a bed, considering the sexual connotations and everything, so I sat near the foot of the bed, the farthest distance from the doctor's chair. Putting my hand on the cold metal frame, I was comforted by its solidity.

I summoned up what interest remained in the topic after the barrage of real-life cases, in order to stimulate the energy needed for the conversation.

"To begin with," I said, to get things rolling, "can you tell me the official diagnosis of the patients I visited today?"

"The first patient, 'Reginald Periwinkle,' has classic delusion of grandeur, a full-blown or 'florid' case.

"Second was Gary Tuttle, a case of paranoid psychosis; he was diagnosed with dementia praecox as a teen and has been institutionalized all his life.

"Third, Scott Milner suffers a unique form of body delusion I have termed geosomatism; I'm working on a paper about it, since it's almost unheard of.

"George Bain, the 'Professor,' is schizophrenic; he thinks he's a history professor at a university, but in fact he never graduated from high school and only worked as a janitor before his breakdown.

"Next was David Singer, who has an unusual form of eratomania, where the patient usually imagines that a celebrity is in love with them.

"Bob Crabtree, or God, is another florid case of grandeur, with manic depression.

"Finally, the patient across the hall" (his door had been closed) "suffers from OCD or obsessive-compulsive disorder and catatonia. He will often spend hours in that same position we left him in.

"So what do you think about our patients, Alan?"

I gathered my thoughts for a moment.

"Earlier, you said that the hallmark of psychosis was not being able to tell the difference between the real and the imaginary. But it seems to me that most so-called 'healthy' people live in their own imagination most of the time – or at least in a mental construct. They may be operationally in touch with their immediate surroundings, but their contextual conception of what's going on is based on information provided by culture, society.

"When you think about it," I continued, "what's 'normal' is deluded, neurotic, compulsive, psychotic, out of touch, living in a mental and false phenomenal world –"

"What's that?" the doctor interrupted.

"False phenomenal world: they don't realize their perceptions are projected outward," I explained with pride.

He made a note and I went on.

"They have unrealistic concepts or fantasies about love, marriage, war... and they are guided by those false conceptions.

"There's rampant repression and filtering based on fear. Repetitive behavior, obsessive behavior. Belief in the supernatural – despite evidence. Rejection of science – which is evidence. Biggest of all: the denial of death... It's folie à deux at the mass level!

"In summary, the psychology of 'most people' seems to match the symptoms of mental illness."

The doctor was not unfamiliar with the argument.

"But you do see the difference, don't you – between real and imaginary, between normal and abnormal, between 'most people' and the patients you met today?"

"Between real and imaginary – yes; between normal and abnormal – yes, but there are gray areas because there's no adequate definition of normal; between 'most people' and your patients – yes, I do see the difference, but only as extremes on a continuum. As far as you can tell from the outside, 'most people' seem normal, but you have to wonder what is going on inside – emotional turmoil, strange thoughts..."

At this point I felt a sudden, almost crippling fatigue. My tank was empty: I was too tired to think anymore. Fortunately, the doctor sensed it.

"Okay, that's enough for today. You need a rest, so we'll give you something to relax you."

Dr. Guilder watched with a smile as Arnold administered the injection, then they went out.

As I relaxed I looked around the room. They had been considerate enough to place my notebook and pen on the desk. Behind the door, on the floor, was a beat-up old brown suitcase with a red handle. I looked at it for some time before recognizing it as my own.

The orderly closed the door.

4

Manikin
Peter Dubé

> "The noble mannequin? [...] She is too untamed to resign
> herself to roles of pure display and attitudes with no resonance."
> René Crevel

It's like this: the margins filled first. My peripheral vision was seized by strange patterns of pale, yet vivid, filigree – what looked like a metallic curtain wavering just out of sight. Then the margins of my notebooks were colonized by the same stuff as I compulsively doodled during meetings and lectures. I drew strange lines and shapes that intersected and overlapped; they weren't letters, nor were they geometrical things either, and despite that they seemed full of import, as if they sought, not so much to represent, as to mean. That's why I kept laying down one shape after another along either side of a page on which I was also writing notes with simpler significance. I can't recall where the enigmatic signs came from, when I might have seen them. I thought there was no connection between the optical phenomena and my new odd behaviour. Now, however, I am wondering.

I'm wondering about this today because I find myself caught, stopped mid-step and held captive by a strange world under glass: a store window. The store is long abandoned; cobwebs have claimed the corners and edges of the vitrine. The webs run along the space's frontiers and spread above a thick layer of dust. The window obviously hasn't been touched for some time, and it isn't much of a display. The merchandise must have been removed months ago when the shop was abandoned. There is nothing to sell here, nothing with a price tag, but for some reason one thing still holds the desolate space: a solitary mannequin.

The figure seems to be male; he is broad through the shoulders, narrow at the hips and muscled in the arms and torso. A strange dark fabric, moiré patterned in a way that suggests reptile skin, is knotted round the waist obscuring the genital area.

That isn't what stops me late in the afternoon and tangled in the lengthening shadows. No, it is the mannequin's surface, his "skin," that fascinates me; he is covered in lines and glyphs too. They are a deep blue, nearly black, colour. The pattern runs up and down his arms and legs, coils around his torso and spreads up either side of the neck to vanish behind the ears. The angle of my view allows me to see nothing more than that. The signs are fascinating; they are the camouflage on some predatory animal, some mathematical progression, some system. I cannot know, but I can't bring myself to look away from the decorated figure. I keep searching for intention, a meaning. My gaze runs from the blank, motionless face to the tips of the toes. There, I see tracks in the accumulated dust: other lines, probably the traces of some finger or some tool. Those lines run in spirals from the window's corners and all lead to the strange, tattooed mannequin's feet. Regular but not facile – like the mannequin's own markings – the dust and the patterns in it seem a map, or a model of some other level of existence.

Why can't I stop staring at this thing?

....

Eventually, by a sheer act of will, I tear my gaze from the strange tableau. I run my errands, including a trip to the jeweller where I leave an heirloom watch to be repaired; the hands have been trapped at eleven o'clock for weeks: time is fettered in a golden frame. A gift returned to me by a lover months ago, after I caught him in a betrayal; our relationship was complicated, but there were some rules to the game. He forgot them, and I am trying to forget him.

The jeweller's establishment is complicated as well: a long, narrow space lined with counters and filled with sparkling things and security cameras. Inside, one always feels as if one were being watched. One is. Even entering is a challenge; I pass through a pair of doors that must be buzzed open.

On leaving I repeat the process backwards, and it seems longer. The first door clicks at my back. Now, standing on the sidewalk as the daylight fades I can hear the second one fall shut. I turn around; it is closed. I walk away; it's almost dark and I want to get home. It's been a strange day.

At the corner, a crossroads, it seems to me I can still hear the buzz letting someone else into the shop. But that can't be right.

....

Last night's sleep was as weird as the day was. It's messing with my head; I can't even remember how I got to this park, but it has been a trying afternoon and I am warm and comfortably sleepy under a tree. I'm seated in long, cooling grass as a bright autumn moon is

40

just beginning its flight towards the zenith. There is the thrum of insects in the air; I'd say they were cicadas but the timing is wrong.

I could sit here all night, looking out at the ridge that rises slowly opposite me; the long slope of lawn marks the boundary of this park, which gives the whole neighbourhood its name. Its rich greens are deepened by moonlight and the curious violet cast creeping into the sky. The chromatic event is cut short by a bolt of lightning. A jagged white slash tears through heaven and vanishes. Then another. Then a brief darkness.

As the light comes back I see something unexpected: a tall figure, naked with a rag wrapped around his waist, his yellowed waxy skin covered in strange dark glyphs, crosses the ridge. His arms are raised above his head, motioning to the sky. His gait and pace are formal in obscure ways. He moves for the far side with great deliberation. Then, as he reaches the end another identical figure appears and begins to cross with equally ritual movements. Then another.

I get to my feet and shake my head. I feel compelled to leave. I turn toward the path out of the park and am stopped by the long, pale, heavily tattooed arm that reaches out; the mannequin master of the dusty window is waiting for me, a doppelganger of the procession at the top of the slope. His mouth twists as if he were wrestling with speech.

I shut my eyes and try to hold back the scream welling in my chest. I shake my head and open my eyes once more to find myself coated in sweat, bolt upright in bed with my curtains undulating in a weak nighttime breeze.

....

When I left work this afternoon, I left behind any certainty about how the world operates. Superficially speaking, nothing unusual happened, not at first; I took the elevator down and hit the street, but when I crossed the four lanes of traffic onto which the building gives I was stopped in my tracks by another shop window. This one fronted a hip clothing designer's place, one whose market is composed largely of angelic-looking young men that spend too much time in nightclubs. There among the fine-lined trousers and the boisterous prints, the fitted jackets and the shoes was my illustrated mannequin: nearly naked, marked with signs, silent. I was trapped again, a prisoner of my fascination and I was frightened. Sweat took my back. What was it doing here? I wanted to go in and ask some member of the staff about it, but was uncertain of the answer, so I didn't. I sped down the street. Headed for the abandoned shop where all of this began. Or did it?

41

I was there in no time, frozen by the mannequin, still, rising above the dust and detritus. But now his arms reach for the glass separating us, for me. I long for him to have eyes, so I can look into them. Instead, I drop my own; see the patterns in the dust again, the accumulation of infinitesimal waste and insect remains. The paths tracking through it tug at me. I follow their winding across the wooden slats and – suddenly – see great branching structures that are half-way between architecture and arbour, clusters of unequal spheres bound together by ridges, branches, what might be bridges. Swirling islands with tufts and tendrils. Grey, pale blue, white. Bizarre centres of power, tightly bound and yet expanding in a web of nearly branch, almost vine. Unbound matter. In one spot, the forms take a nearly spherical shape I cannot begin to explain. Any more than I can what seem to be nascent crystals in some corners of the massive, emergent world. Everywhere, there is the suggestion of new matter, of the formless taking on form: protostructures, the barest hints of what-might-become-walls. Mating obelisks. The walls of possible-palaces. Towers and pits. But foetal stars and toddler nebulae as well. The suggestion that the beginning of the material is coterminous with its end. And there is a vast chittering sound too; the source of it is ferociously indeterminate. It may be to my left, my right. Overhead perhaps. But on intuition, I choose to spin around. Behind me, a pair of enormous crustacean claws emerges from a burgeoning cluster of tendrils and turrets. A mite of some kind, but visible to me at thousands of times its normal size. It shocks me back to ordinary consciousness. A fall through darkness, or a floating away.

I walk from the window; I must reject its proliferating universe, its soup of signs.

....

I have a few drinks and ignore the memories of the dilating microscopic world. I let the television run for both the auditory and the visual noise. At length, I go to bed.

Now, I repose in the dark. Recline: let the tension seep from my muscles, try not to chase after rest, hope that it will come on its own. Instead, a pattern of coruscating colour whirls on the ceiling, keeping me awake. But none of it ever takes on a fixed shape, ever means anything recognizable. Despite this, I track each flash; ignore the weight I'm beginning to feel beside me. The mattress is sinking but I will not look; then there is a presence beside me, a feeling of partial substance. Until it grows firm. Like flesh, only cool. I can't tell whether this new thing rises from the bed itself or has precipitated itself out of the atmosphere. And a hand falls on my stomach; I turn. He is here. His skin covered in the sigils that begin to flash as he rolls

42

atop me: the mannequin now in motion. His head reaches towards mine; new lips part and a tongue enters my mouth with a subtlety I don't expect. I can feel his breath flow into me, mine into him. There is no fabric round his loins now and though I know there should be no cock there I can feel it hardening against my own. His hands run down my body; he is here past the doubting. He turns his head for a moment. I can see the glyphs written into the flesh of his neck twist as he grinds himself against me; their curves and angles lengthen, flexing as his fingers slide down to grasp my buttocks. His mouth comes back to mine. The colours overhead have not rested from their swirling and they call to the phantom, phantasmatic spectra in my own mind with a force like gravitation. A sound like music. The mannequin looks into my eyes with a terrible focus in the still blank spaces of his sockets. The right hand on my buttocks slides into the cleft. Strokes against my asshole. A wall of red, yellow, blue inside my head cracks open, the force tears open the polychromatic sky on my ceiling; tattering it. A newborn mountain rears up in the flux of accelerated time and space. The hieroglyphic mannequin kisses me again; spreads my legs. And I respond to him; my hands run across his decorated back, slide around his waist. My left hand finds his impossible erection. Finds it already moist with some lubricant. Above the emergent mountain scarlet tinged clouds have begun to gather as a sun dips below the horizon; they toss great bolts of lightning between them that never touch the ground. My breath stops for a second as I see slight figures quit the clouds and begin to swirl in the gathering storm. I kiss the mannequin again and again as he positions himself between my thighs. Thunder seizes my visionary room carrying shrill laughter in its wake. The clouds broil as a blood stained moon parts the army of cumulonimbi. Terrifying women and ragged men with hypertrophied erections, too-long arms and scrotums through which one can see potential creatures sleeping in the seminal fluid ride the sound. The lightning is echoed; there are minute flashes in the void-sockets of my lover's eyes as two of the signs marking his flesh – half circles with radiant arrowheads – slide into place on his brow. I can feel his cock pressing against me and with a shock of cold, or is it heat, or is it both, he is inside of me. My mouth opens in pain, but I cannot find my voice: instead a peel like brazen bells rocks the room as his hips begins to move. Red lightning and blue now. A twister of flying figures takes shape: they chant words I cannot recognize in a rhythm that shakes me to my core. As the man-mannequin fucks me the signs and symbols on his skin begin to flow across his form quicker and quicker. Turning and churning like the angry elements. As he pulls me against him, he

43

bends down to kiss and to lightly bite my nipple and I acquiescence, every cell of my skin trembling for him. As his lips reach me, a glyph that looks like a stroke of celestial fire slides from his chin and onto my chest. It feels cool as it takes root. From the thumb grasping my waist I see an inverted triangle with what might be a spider at its heart creep from him and make for my inner thigh. I can't watch anymore so I close my eyes and feel him fuck me with an irregular rhythm and a vast intensity. Something begins to rise from a newly exposed cavern at the summit of the mountain: something with great wings that seem to gather up the clouds. I can feel my lover grasp me tighter, I can feel new things moving on the surface of my body that seem to be meaningful, and I can feel my own cock swelling, building towards its climax. The mannequin's breath, is it breath? is in my ear and I hear a word, nothing I expected, a word: "simultaneity."

I finally shout. I bolt up; there is no man between my legs. Nothing inside me, but I am sweaty, and dizzy, and delirious with an incomprehensible pleasure. The clock reads 4:30 AM. I am alone. I cannot account for any of this, any more than I can explain my fading erection or the semen drying on my belly.

....

What place is this? Where might I be? Regardless of what I see. All sensation set aside; there is no way to know I am not asleep in my bed right now, immersed in dreams. There is no overwhelming reason to claim any of this is real. To claim any of this is not. There is no reason. I shut my eyes, hoping to awaken when I open them again. When I do. Where am I?

....

I evade. I evoke. I walk a long, circuitous path. I pace completely around several blocks in turn, simultaneously heading towards and avoiding my destination: the dust-caked window that separates, or separated, me from the hermetic mannequin. Every step puts me in mind – once again – of wind and thunder. Where there is none. Now.

Standing before the plate glass I see what must be the mannequin, but it is shrouded in a pale drop cloth and bound in white rope; the lengths and coils of it crossing and crisscrossing the shape and echoing the signs, I know, I hope, are still on his form. Even worse, the shrouded form has grown, is nearly double in volume, as if he held another person in an invisible embrace. As if there were two bodies underneath that covering.

In the flat light I can see my own reflection swim across the glass. Whether it is on the outer surface, searching for a way in, or on the inner, struggling for egress is impossible to say.

44

I am awake I tell myself. I reach out to the glass; I want to be sure of it. My sleeve rides up and on my wrist, in blue ink and black a mark that shouldn't be there: an oscillation of dark lines, almost circular – it could be two shells, or twin moons meeting in eclipse, a pair of eggs left in sunlight and forgotten, matched eyes coming together for a new kind of vision, dual shields hung on a waxy yellow wall after the battle has been won, the monument to the memory of a royal couple who oversaw the abolition of an earlier language and instated new symbolic systems, a pair of cephalopods rising to the surface, game pieces and so much more. A trick of the light; the sheet over the mannequin seems to move.

And a powerful wind comes out of nowhere and batters at the window, rattles it in its frame. It beats against my shaking hand.

5

Six Poems
Anatoly Kudryavitsky

The Batless Batman

I am dressed in someone snug. It may be you,
with your watchful makeup and exaggerated (s)laughter.

Questions ask me questions.
Who did I spider but a yucca Spanish lady?
What did I get but a cobwebbed kiss?
In which "before" have I been before,
at the dawn of the sky tomato?

I used to naught where it was hot.
I pleated my shadow over the fleeting universe.
Was I ill in a suit – or just ill-suited?

These days I live the chequered street
named after José Ambrosio Tinto de Verana
a.k.a. Josip Broz Tito.
I am still veranifying the name.
My "very" is a very wary "very."
When thirsty, I drink my television.
It says I have a stupor power.

The bird of yes tweets no. The sky water,
the order of its ripples.
The odour of "stay recovered."

In Our Tribe

Sunburst pebbles, pure bramble light
leaching the legends...
The flower of the hour unfolds,
then folds again; the loudspeaker exhales
less and less daydreams.
Even words come to an end.

The story has a mind of its own.
Magician's hands unveil the cabinet of fog.
Face the space.
Face the pace of the *Pax Oceanica*.
Is there something striving to conquer us
through the back door?

Bad luck is sticky as a muck creek.
History is only trying to help.
Talk to my war paint, to my plumbic plumage.
Three elders bubble at the very
surface of sense.
"How long is this light for?" asks the darkness.

Errant

Talking furniture can be a bit furry
but generally it's OK. *Amerikanisch*.
I once approached the outer wall,
but it didn't let me through
into general oxygen.
What else are walls for? Or publishing outlets?

Cloud water, our petrol...
Say hello to the world's dust;
ring blaze bells for the miles.
There's something new on the menu:
a kick-off of confidence, boldness bolsters.
Let's make the word "great" great again.

Who wears the slumber of temples?
I wear daybreak and twilight; grammarians
are bedizened with leprechaun green.
The globe's delusions rest upon creaky
roof beams. Where else but in this picture?
When, if not now?

Language juices get sticky.
Who will juice out into Mistake woods
where trees wear *Native-Born* badges
on their lapels?

No mistakes here. No woods either.
My aura is verdant; it is spreading.
This frightens me:
man must keep his aura
close to his skin.

Eva / *Ewig*

Winged plums, tearful potatoes;
the de-adornment of a portrait...
Your drum is a dream, your bell
winds the woods,
villages of darkness.

You come in, sit down.
A shaky evening, a flaked mistake.
Our branches, yours and mine, are
thoughts of the same tree.
Who's crying so micaceously?

I exit. I come back in.
The bell that winds the village,
the woods of darkness.
Talking flowers, I am tired of you.
Cats and kitchens scare me immensely.

The vitality of Evita
between the sound and frozen holiness.
Loving is living your life backwards.
You bathe your indifference
in the blue pool of white.

Baleen Blubber

Whale whiffling, baleen blubber...
Language is a difficult thing to fin
into your mouth. Place your knowledge
in the discovery position.

Even if wafted into wackiness, we
string our strengths.
Our blood-coloured loves,
our salty ears, crystallising

upon our shoulders...
I wanted to dive into escapism,
I really did. Barbadian crabs bubbled me
out of it.

On my left is a cleft stick, on my white
a night. Algae go algebraic.
Our hopes, the black shades of crimson.
Our tomorrows dressed in oversight.

The Lenses of Asclepius

Heart filled with pride is a wooden flower.
Celestial rectos and versos
in the early light of opportunity,
droplets of the native shore...
Salt on heaven's lips, who will read it?

The century has been launched
by the crime of the century.
Enforce the law of your trivia.
There's always room for corraborators.
The world is still not "world" enough.

Soft-fingered skills... It is so precipitative
to make plans...
The weather forecast is the end of all weather,
and the master escapist jitters into a helplessness dance
with a glass statue.

Funeral threads. More funeral threads.
Grimaces call themselves mirrors.
In the clouds, a private eye looks into the case
through the tearful lenses of Asclepius.
His brain is rain.

6

Two Poems
John M Bennett

mot muet

mot muet

utilance tra asses - *C. Mehrl Bennett*

𝕄 𝕄 𝕄 𝕄 𝕄 𝕄 𝕄 𝕄 𝕄 𝕄

sənd
əmıp
ɹoʇ
ɒnd ʇs
bıd
ɯɹoɟ
ɥsɒɹʇ
ʇs əəp
ʇnb

went wet in suit after wind   coffed out ah
corner pocket   it's yr heaving in meat umbrella
furled back yr behind   was is
chewed on the ice mask   slide into lens

Then therefore was swallowed now
The toad by White Life.
- *Popol Vuh*

           forend caps crux neck fog noose binst comb
        rinsed cluub moll   ember in the door   re
    ach it hole cluster   beel at sslumber nostrill was
       wwind poulet   LeLogg cambera mot mote
         iittcchh hhoott bboooomm it when   hall
         collabpsed the rend   's near heard unhung
                a bend for slab foreslabt

))last rasping gasp   floor rest
rustling hands   node clock belching smoke
on a mute mat was   it torn
now then never edge isn't   ....dull...........
throaty   white tongue   curled in an ear
ate a fly   saw animolds we   a stab rune the is(((

𝐌UTE MOT MOTE ETOM TOM ETUM

fought and burned

John M. Bennett

1.9.19

las llamas de la bruna

las llamas de la bruma

...vimos a la Pelona bajo la sombra de un tenderete.
- Roberto Bolaño

))o hole relentless clouding breath collapsant
grill my clog usher in nor fork nor laundry
shout *What* from the other room(((

> *dream of old naked women in a barber shop*
> *is a dream of a ship at sea wide flat deck*
> *covered with birds and basket balls dream of a*
> *ship is the dream of a tunnel carved into a*
> *mountain ends at a lake of mercury and c*
> *offee g rounds*

TORMENTA GLOTOLÚLICA

insane the fog insane the light insane the
bathroom sink insane the short-sleeved shirt

insane the nahui4 **T**ezcatlipocas insane the elbow
insane the watch insane the gristle shining

in dark above the **bèd**

> *a dusty sandwich swivels toward your face p*
> *late of wind a is ,the eat wind ,chain inversion it*
> *chair a gelatinous retch time was cold cuts to*
> *floor fall ,slips in   other face   frog wheel*
> *in asleep*

///[RATIONAL FOG LASSITUDE

clustered nape before uh mirror close door the
///[pills headache wh whisspers in ay ear ay ears a
y ear ly mild ew blooms face yr thumping shadow]]]]

>BAM BBAAMM BBBBAAAMMM BBBBAAAAMMMM

MMMMMMMMMMMMMMm <

"DRAIN THE ICE YOUR HAND FORGOT"

la loma pelada la lona meada la pielona
al anoleip *LA PELONA LA PELONA*
l'appelona l'appeluna l'appeloca
¿ppor qué me llamas?

John M. Bennett   2.16.19

7

A Story and a Poem
Dale Houstman

The Fair Inconstant

No room service until poetry is the bell.

.

Writing is rude to interrupt what might otherwise be a life of pure insensibility.

.

Beauty is more and less a cautious species of vacancy.

.

Distance is fate's makeup.

.

Culture is an enormous elaboration into which the Beautiful has fallen and cannot get up.

.

Absolution is murder with guilt as the innocent party.

.

Most people live *somewhere in the neighborhood* of themselves.

.

Rudeness is the Revolution of the momentary.

.

No matter how little we actually move, science will never catch us.

.

Spit will not kill a priest, which is why so few are spat upon. Try it anyway...

.

Once the Tiger becomes smoke, no cigarette is safe.

.

Light arrives from our eyes. The sun soaks in it.

.

Candles are light determined to be *conducted*.

.

> Only a blind man's body supports the head as water supports the jellyfish; the senses are heavy in the head, but light in the body.

.

Consciousness is a rank privilege.

.

The mind contains the body. All else is the Great Outdoors.

.

The absurd is *never* ridiculous.

.

One might as well sweat ashes as pearls.

•

You never step in the same river twice. But it's always wet.

•

The water's sensuous dialectic merely imitates fish.

•

Chess is the *operatic arm* of Tic Tac Toe.

•

Almost everyone you meet looks like a violent peacock.

•

The moon is a peasant's idea of philosophy, and—since the moon appears to agree with this
estimation—the idea is deemed fully sufficient.

•

Night is sweetened by kings, but it is peasants who get the toothaches.

•

      No matter how many trees you fold in your handkerchief each
evening, morning will find you
lost in the woods.

•

Nature is always full.

•

Every red flower owns a ghost who bleeds into it. Every white flower freezes
its ghost into view.
Every blue flower arches above in observation. Every flower in your mouth is
a bouquet for
Stalin.

•

Our breaths are like imprecise notebooks.

•

This world is not interesting enough to be singled out as dull.

•

Dissolution is an unvocalized desire for an ideal reunion.

•

Candles are light determined to be conducted.

•

I know nothing but what is extinguished

•

You came to buy candles, but you'll settle for a moth.

•

Resignation is the poor man's happiness.

•

Dark hair precipitates its face. Blond hair *debuts* its face.

•

Things change, but the wait can kill you.

•

Waffles are pancakes with modernist structural pretensions... If you like waffles, you yearn for a Cartesian regularity to your life to balance your internal "scrapple" turmoil. You wish most of all to wander a nicely arranged labyrinth in search of Frank Lloyd Wright. You abhor the way spaghetti mimics your consciousness and dream of the day Malevich's "White Square on White" opens its linear heart to you and makes everything efficient, clean, and easy to absorb through your simple crystalline pores. You not only do not want to live "off the grid" you desire to move permanently into the center of the Great Griddle, where the Art Deco Elves are vanquishing the Art Nouveau faerie folk. Oh, and the sun is square...

A Sort of Take Away (Echo Board Warehouse)

A carnival abortion would have been more celebrated. In trying to be a clear bell and not allow access to the essential asexual cavity that is a nation and its towns, we viewed ourselves as an echo of white noise from a passing construct, an idea train without freight. Never mind the initial point which keeps moving away from the overeager human program. So... as the *alluring scene* was a semantic substitute for that asexual cavity and the white noise in terminal transit... so was our singular question not toned to imply the audience, or to excrete a way forward, or even the understood incapability of either. Plenty to go around. Wrapped in thin allotments. The imagination's souvenir ashtray.

The fetters of starlings about the captured taxonomy merely a burble now of illicit pretext and the *anti-centrality of the under-dialogue.* Inhuman contact expressed through earnest luminaries, contracted to a mind in a felt of responses, a rubber throttle on our query: *why bother to argue the point*? Exhaustion manifold. Spring in an abandoned pie.

Is this desperation a thumbnail of a *hot-mind application* which by profit is numbed by our slight gestures? Or... as gesture are not determined by past debt... only an arbitrary trap with the *experiential mimicry* to generate randy freedom? Well, there are factors we know but will not sentimentalize for sale. Humans... That fashionable homework debris in which *the lever of removal* was bonded with a drab tin honey bucket, deep as money so we could not see the bottom's circle of adders. *"An admission: we were not looking for that midget dream house bloodied down its legs,"* a tidy sun embedded in our eyes puled. Pale the tiger athwart the pyramid of revolutionary dental metal. Trigger those shiny implements of a toy slavery mechanism to pin the town center to a trajectory. *"Things should be done by things, so don't get me started,"* The tiny embedded sun puled.

Is it now calling us? Come, tyrant and thug and be well served by a consummation of democracy upon the blanket. No, it is not calling us. From the prettiest wounds caressed by a disturbed boy we infer a hidden document smelling of a senator ripe caressing in turn *the sword of civil progress.* Was this the slaughter of poetry? No overt trip switches? No cuter tools? In this same fashion love is excused from condensation. There is a street, there is a pole, there is a tower of tires. Each is a center of closeted loyalty or invoked mummery. And so on, and so on… Cue.

In part because people assume they know what *it* is, what *it* is capable of, and exactly how they *possess it*. The assumption is a fade into sincerity, and though we race to the community theatre, a lack finishes first. At this point observation becomes needy, a black hole inside a black hole inside an economy of desire. The austerity of the unfree. A tape loop of *geared pining*.

Or are they also being programmed to spew agitating resistance, *the what-we-got* counterpoints *the indiscernible ration*? No… their nature succumbs to our *gas of brilliance*. We are their retirement home, their final solace in the arms of disregard. The answer remains "no." But you cannot trust even that cogency, that attractive brevity.

Through naïve and leisurely, I fear love is a company which personalizes hope to make it ownable. Programming itself is afloat in our remains: a film of *victimless information*. The relative disappointment is absorbed in an artificial and effortlessness of surface, *the revealed anything*.

The poverty of the latent poetry hastened by conduction. Or is there no such thing as conduction? If not why will existence render an inside and an outside of situations? We are living through *the revealed anything*, which is both exhilarating and depressing: exhilarating the sea changes, depressing in happenstance.

In *the insidious there*, a privilege to watch a criminal turn autumnal, and a rifled dream of corporate girls no longer homesick for the bogwash, *the revealed anything* is found by tracking its seeping and sighs, both quieted by whatever absorbed the fun. Fun has been had. There is an ugly floor beneath the pretty carpet we must imagine… And soon a bride left at the abattoir speaks of the pleasures of a long-lost high school band. The brass of pride.

The State has the mood spectrum of a goldfish and its cities beckon no one. There are those who cannot see a binary star in the pile of tires. Those who shoot pearls of blither up the sweet moaning air of urgency opiated. Who are our unloved, distant consorts, the howler monkeys here and there disguised as the well-intentioned revolution of the trepanned swans and the violated houseplants? Were we there to hear the bellowing of a wildebeest being run over by a steam engine? And did we? We do not remember who served it to us. The program shall be hollowed out and labeled as *a corrupted fact paste*, our last remaining collop, as if a lever had been scraped out of us and pulled so that our eyes, no matter where we stood, or how we push it see only the shabby curtains of optimistic ignorance.

8

Night Feeding
J. Karl Bogartte

"We have come then to this place to dissolve rebelliously, and with irony, to share our ferrous grids and molecular hives, our absolute flesh colors and porous identities drawn by shadows, slashed by hunger. In this we are ageless quartz."

*

The double-faced window of a highland arc, the fearless one, the Archeologist with larval-smoke and teetering, she gestured... She swallows and glows from within. Throws the first fire, with pitchfork urges. Troubles the lorn, translates into aspects of incendiary and babbling, coupling a shadow. You project accommodation with ambiguity and a penchant for heuristic pendulums. Desire is a flash fire clothed in dusk.

*

Pleasure is a paradoxical axon to the annotators of language. You have long since lowered your resistance to myelin milkweed and the splendid solace of a torch, bleeding a constellation whenever possible. For what unnamed street introduces a midnight stroll in phosphorus and synapses, and the word *corona* overrun with crying machines and sinister keys searching for hidden locks.

*

In delirium there is ample room for the illusion of pleasu re, the black flower   of night. The nitro of love's glycerin in the warehouse of mannequin s...

*

There are beautiful engines barricading the streets, soft and liquid bestiaries, sirens of anatomical window-games. At the edge of time the elder's lens appears without hesitation, sharing conundrum and pineal gland melodies. For a seasonal molting, to replace not the bees spinning their sheets of glass, but the Keepers dreaming that *once upon a time* will come, heavy with bells flourishing inside the starlight ovens. Shaping lead into fusible gifts. Replace the words with shrieks of nightingales, beneath the skin, startled, lightning shaped. Fluorite-enabled. Transparent as water. Missing in Peru...

*

By animal warmth and eyelight, shaking the heron rattle in the lightning bed, cutting night into ladders and depth of field. The entrances grow further apart, the others growing more ambiguous, raising a deeper turbulence of instinct... To mingle with fury, elasticity for the body's aboriginal web.

*

She is morphos, turning blue between layers of turbulence. The flares projecting repeated whispers, igniting each portrait in many places at once, a woman, river, drinking, countless clues in accidental places. Instability leaves a trace of candles and reckless conjuration. Precious mint is always the presence of a scissors in the darkness of love.

*

The image without reason is an exception to the rule. The plural is placenta of imaginary vibrato, droning. She is the image, undoing, consumed, spitting image. You are the gatherer, the state of being actively offered, for mirroring, dark matters, wolf-lamp for breathing, double voice for an evening chamber, liminal threshold, a negative light and a mouthful... image to shun, to cabal, interface for schemes to sharing blood and fire, in bewildering chiaroscuro... The image is your body grazing for immoral rumors in the carcass-driven desert of oneiric anomalies, silvering, desaturation, a shadow-dance of altered neurons. You shift among images, radiant plume.

*

To repeat "I have not forgotten the arc that shapes to the whirling shadow of things, I am a part of your reflections..." *from them,* where random animals stoop to bathe, shedding sparks... and the dark flood fills outward your *hop, skip and a jump.* But only facing behind where it is known, "the brides come and go like pinnacles" and insect time is murmuring, voices humming, splattering... "Configure your messages to meet me in morning light, where the messengers are out of touch..." Rubbing and fingering for unheard-of desire.

*

An ongoing and fierce night of women out of desert sand, between no other hands, anarchy and metamorphosis to always be announced, with fraud and butterfly signals. Password for a cyber-sphinx is a midnight gambol, a last remark that appears as heavy as anything loved, disgraced and criminal. Hands that glow and rig themselves to the starry corner of a room, to give birth, to sputter and hammer into a single spark, into the twilight of a revolving door that resembles in all respects, the vast expanse of your ribcage and esplanade... Making bright things out of sand smeared with night...

*

You wax rapidly for the melody of a precocious schism wrapped up, like a waterfall, in a gown-dragon for the librarian's table. A lunar-fiddling dream. The unsettling geometry of a superb marksman. A doorway of calipers.

*

Almandine, sister of Mint, the little savage. She befriends a tossup of angular rags, polishing triangular surfaces of Opia and Oneida into a night-harp. Slipping through a morii keyhole, ending a very long sentence for a moment of whispering between walls. The Cabal of Aurora, sending x-rays into a séance of perfect gestures...

*

The eel-headed sentry, half painted and fabric of shadow, a sundial reservoir. To denounce the unavoidable, to quiver it. Meticulous piecing together all that cannot be, seen, the arc-gathering mirage in albino headdress. Maya in acrobatics, shape-brandishing the sense of somatic veils bursting open in the garden. The envy of a tumultuous root system, turning windows in the desert. To feed the silence with ions and spores, a spinning top of chemical reactions, and that "have we met before?" smeared across many years of a stone's throw away from presence and absence. Sleeping together. A flood of particles...

*

A multiple of appearances in one swoop, a bright bewildering narrative. Assyrian veils torn to shreds, for wings, "I am your lamp, your moth antennae and voice. I am the sling-blade of conspirators, the warm tenderness of mumbling. A veil of ashes, a jealously guarded instrument of surprise..." Each indefinable gesture relives those flowering schematics for tilting the principle point of tension between a phantom space and the live dream, between the eyes... one hovering body over another, rapturous theories of seduction beyond the point of no return.

*

Flood, intoxication of the wolf-crystal, she is everywhere. A marvelous moisture. Scent understands you, follows your patterns of behavior. Drawn to what enables your defiance, figures of celluloid and slate and womb-like chairs invading your appearance. Long-haired and spindle-bursting for Flood who slumbers in the arms of Ghostly Apparel who burns brightly with Morphology. They are the whispers of default, litter of early rising dew. "Only shadows allowed in this place...

*

Night in braille, poison and antidote for a hybrid of black and flower slashed by ultraviolet. To breathe clairvoyance through stone, speaking in tongues to the lost fingerprints traveling incognito towards daybreak. A single image replaces your history with layers of silence turned by paws into unrecognizable balconies. Light speaks, night listens. Pearls circling a miasma of gestures seeking an entrance.

*

For intoxication, there is fur for the enchanter's tower, facial-lepidoptera for pelvic charm, dimensional collusion to enrich your brow of forgotten plumage. What is remembered is the irritation of possibility. The sting of dark perception. Primal movement, irresistible language pulled out of water for flame... What is recognizable as something, is unrecognizable as other, into another. The mind is like the irritability of a missing limb. Language is the missing body. Breathing is the enchantment of movement. Plumage is formidable...

*

The angora of perception rings a bell, raising the tables with ghostly stakes. You listen to the accents for tutelage of resuscitation, and you flood with tinctures and pigments glowing awkwardly in latent messages. Against the wall, the hummingbird sewing machine plays havoc with your presence, activating webs of a time-lapse pulled up out of the earth through your eyes.

*

Somewhere, light on a mirror points to a shadow, that knows you intimately, always finds you, like one breath finds another, the pleasure of struggling enacts a corona of debatable lampposts. A fierce theory of magical properties brightly growing out of ontic fabulations and erotic intercessions, polished to last a lifetime, like a herd of traveling clocks. It cannot be avoided. Those interposing conundrums in search of the most precious stones.

*

A mumbling savant keeps the chronologists at bay, takes apart those lost Arabic consternations, planting morning glories for clarity. A love-sick girl who is perpetually lighting candles... A sorceress without mercy, with training wheels for archival balance. Your transparency enables that luminosity of over-riding concerns, being seen through, for a vast landscape that doesn't know you. But who you are. The absurd brilliance of reinhabiting your body with no precedent. Mumbling... Imprinting...

*

Solanace was gathered for the delight of Loon, heavily veined for an eager eclipse, glyphing in turbulence. A ragged occultation, romance of the fetching water-carrier. Fingering roses for taste and ignition, persistent scythe in analogue, as the homeless beggar of imaginary conjuration. Even movement dreams, through dimensional spaces. Kissing Loon, spilling mint, eating Solanace...

*

Entering through the wild sibilance of Mayan throats, anterior shades of lightning, texts for the forest creatures to continue their librations, their theater curtains and long lost gestures found only in phantom stones. Filled with bright blood. In the film you disappeared behind the camera. Undressing fruitless poses. Consternation and melancholy opening doors, to open landscapes, opening light, arousing a dark sequence of treasured auburn and hypnotic purring.

*

When the moon is black, the presence of water is bilingual and upright. Flicker was abundant with supernatural distractions. She was a charlatan of pistil and stamen rattling, a clamoring ladder. A pooling ceremony with magical teeth, spitting out highly active words of turbulence. Vespertine adored Flicker and their meetings were never spoken of except in secrecy. They were savages blooming in fragrant bathing suits, in italics and pathological murmurs. They were trumpets of purloining.

*

What is planted in night's belly, a long-tailed grimoire to mink the utterings of minx, dipping underneath, the sundial of enchanted pores. Ghostly personages forced through the space of less time than it takes to either repel them, or give in to their own daylight longing. The watchtower will always remain incomplete, sirens go up in smoke, and your eyelids are flickering madly in the mirror of the aerialists.

Selections from a work in progress.

9

Two Poems
Kirby Olson

THE MUSIC OF MONDO BODIES

The curvature of the great blue whale
the physics of its locomotion
the power of the locomotive
the colossal blimp
a space-station moving through nothing-ness.
A supertanker moving across the Gulf Current
an airplane cutting across a river of air
planets wobbling intermittently in space a
meteor hurtling toward earth, a baby grand
piano (or three!) dropped on Hamden, NY

ARGOS PANOPTICON

I could have been a river
until I heard myself laugh
I could have been a plum
until I drank wine I could
have been a whirling dervish
until I sat before the mirror
I could have been a bean blossom
until I realized I was a butterfly
I could have been a human until
I saw my million convex eyes.

10

A Call to The Unregenerate
AE Reiff

By the time I hear from you I will have forgotten you are there. I want
to tell you I'm waiting for owls with iron feathers, scorpions,
caterpillars, ants turned peacock. It's beautiful if you like the sort.
One society exchanged privileges with another for controls. Don't
have names for them yey, the samurai behind the back, an elbow in a
chair, knee to the left, shoulders right, entities of Collective Mind.
Flies, locusts wade across the mass, poor frog done more harm than
good. It's about never arriving at the state from the one we fled,
rebellious long ears turned into horns in the middle of foreheads,

Elijah the stranger who can see the dementia flat heart fake fire stares. Salvation comes in miniature one ounce packs. Always the same for those on top. The cow was a bear, the cow was a lion, the cow was anything but itself, but nothing compared with the hog hordes that styed the soil so they were more like wolves. rpgs out of their mouths, hot foam from nostrils so much it put out the fires. They were fire pigs that looked like tigers, but at night had pillows for their heads. You think this bad but what about the tens of thousand dogs, one eyed and three legged as myths of Cadmus and Actaeon and GEryon, Cephalus dog, biting among foxes who broke into banks and raided the old S&L safe boxes and ate all the chickens, joined by the cats of Akron. The cats of Akron infest house and barn even as the well to do wonder cock changed with the sheep, all at once incandescent in the yard, blue, gold, scarlet with the sun maybe, except the rooster beak of a falcon took wings, checked every day the progress of the rotting sycamore twenty feet up where grew carpenter bees, big black buzzers to inhabit the cracks and fly the hollowed stump over perhaps every burrow dug by tortoises on a human September grazed lawn. Some turned black as you might imagine, hundreds, thousands copulated in air and on ground.

After enlightenment don't worry, All is One Forbidden, and opinion like weather forecasts, comes in small dreams that belong to someone else. Dreams have significance, but they turned it always worshiping Baal asses in revolt, nothing compared with the cows in feedlots with bear feet and dragon tails, breath so sulphurous it set fire to roofs of those towns. How many ways to pollute thinking? Ophelia silent in the roar. They lived freely when there were images broadcast from a projector and all the authorities of the world were deposed, taken over. This film now showing dressed up dolls with finger rings, that if you live well toward knowing, laugh rivers with people who don't want electricity, whose doubts flood against the Unknown of Idaho, Utah, Nevada, and the Great Basin will not wash away. Physical hardened topographies reinhabit internal species. Civilized boots back Good up the edge down the hill. The road winds and then the truck, backed up and in, bodies in mind piling up fox, bear, seal, hawk, coyote, horse, start to come apart from the unmaking glued back skins, beaded ridges marred as if none, nameless, to look at the **faces** below, diminish plateau, mountain and cave, a topography one can see. The face, the nose, the cheek, the brow that shades the eyes, one knee stuck out, arm down among hunchbacks, joined at the shoulder. One's a girl. The guy's got an arm around her, looking down, praying something. Shoulders, heads, one, two, three long coats, hats on top, left on the rocks. Herringbone moving. Somebody hasn't been born.

People that play with clouds. An eye hidden in a cliff, toddlers in the rocks. The other arm sticking out, you know what that is? A bird on a roost or a fat monk. Ohio long since gone, what seeds do were gone, sown, fallen in a harvest raised against wilderness scab-shriveled mold and armyworm during day winter pupa in soil. Innumerably terrifying monsters various bands of the common through fields changing shapes into wild beasts. In docudramas the trouble comes from women, men, groups, rivals, from the Freedom that makes known those who harbor such thoughts: "this man and woman were the most profoundly beautiful human." That's the adagio.

Elijah said unconscious awake blew everything up. Jars of pickles exploded, spreading over London, no news of Washington, its body parts more seriously spread along. Gofernment cordons, rebreeds it, feeds it. Gogernment opposes. Superpods digest fluorescent mucous with past war sacrifice, all wars against the natural, the self, the other, nothing gorgonment but wars to end them all appeared. Elijah, the man with four last initials had a desk in no building, no desk unless the count books with their spanking covers, books and plants, rue to grow monarchs from chrysalis. So he had a hand in the Gambel quail that took refuge. Salvation miniatures.

The best advice was to go into captivity, swimming underwater in viscose veins, fish with a blemish, tanks to survive a war. Not waiting in Weimar to start, or the wonders of survival in a meat locker under Dresden, sense impressions of the real, or bailing out over Paris, the unreal upstart that can't hear the noise of its own approach, vapor trails of its rockets to deny, chemtrails of a war like ghosts flee the Judean fields. Shouldn't we be doing something, run to the street, warn the others, empty the mind so the cupboard jars don't explode, launch commandos? The fall not yet, you wake up on the coast of a storm and swim out where the sun is having a beautiful day walking in September among comets. King Ranch that overwhelmed the blue stem a century before had nothing to say of captivity, eyes rasping for light, shadows of herd grown great, full length wasted gods rotting in pillows. There would be no common breakfasts or dressing, being without bodies, or cruets, crocks and casseroles in these fantasies of the collective mass corp. So say it for him, Jeremiah to his St. John, over and over state the unobvious gofernment torn page out of this philosophy that burns in the grate. We're going to speak for him a new reality more like a prison cell but without the acrylic intellect of real prisons where inmates know they are incarcerate. These don't know their rations, their cells, their collective tiers, stripes or pink underwear, jostling in the yard with shanks and tools of kindness. Insert the ipad and cell phone and a desktop to flick the microwaves, power earplugs and GPS wandering. Next person up will have memory wipe, rejuvenalization straight, couplets drilled flat, doilies surrogate to live reprogrammed in the heaven applauding episodes that remove anxiety, dreams working late at night to raise eagles and wearing a heavy shirt, a large eagle lands on his shoulder of the life you must know, while a smaller female lands in his lap, profusion of eagles that find the carcass gathering, and a baby eagle snuggles into his fur, the mother preening, while the father with claws next to his neck looks out, as if each were to bring the unique text written burning in acts of precognition, warnings before the fact, with a large white dog or a coyote, a dumpster around the corner he can't see, but knows and if those, St John, de nada, his portals, that hold the blueprints a cappella under the casement, Kyrie Eleison, emaciates come to call sinners not the righteous, light in the dark of Last Words of Babylon.

Ein Ruf an die Unwiedergebohrene Welt
https://matthiasbaumannofoley.blogspot.com

Code of Conduct
Mazduda Hassan

If I were to speak in silence now, I would say this – it is possible to dive into the ocean and become the ocean, to swim with the clouds and become the clouds, to fall into silence and uncover the universal secret.

How? One would ask, then many would ask and to them my answer would remain blank because their question of how did not come from a longing to know the how. For a moment my questioning silence grabbed their attention. Hence they asked to help themselves laugh about it later.

The ones who did not ask but let the silence stand still are the ones to receive my answers. I would of course silently answer to each of their individual's ear so that they would fall into the silence with me and become one with the universal silence of the oceans, earths, and the skies.

This is how silence has been restored since generations.

The First Date
Angel Dionne

He didn't usually invite first dates to his home. But, when he'd met her in the grocery store he knew no other place would do. She didn't seem like the type who would enjoy the theatre nor would she be at ease in a crowded café. And so, he invited her over for afternoon coffee. She stepped into the threshold of his home at exactly one o'clock. She wore her yellow hair loose and was simply dressed in a long skirt and a blue blouse. He made black coffee and set it on the table with small bits of toasted bread and cheese.

I was surprised when you asked me to come over, she said.

How so?

I'm not usually the type to be noticed in a grocery store.

Well, I did notice you. You were buying cabbage, canned soup, and a box of crackers. You wore a white summer-dress with sandals. I noticed a lot.

Her thin bottom lip quivered a bit as she smiled.

So, what do you do?

Nothing right now. I used to be a painter, he said.

Used to? What do you mean, used to?

I mean I no longer paint. I can't paint.

She took a lock of hair and placed it between her lips. She chewed intently as she listened to him. A thin smear of saliva collected in the left corner of her mouth.

That doesn't make much sense to me.

Why not?

Well, you're still a painter even if you don't paint right now. A doctor is still a doctor even if he takes a vacation.

No, you misunderstood. I can't paint.

Can't?

No. I used to paint all the time but something happened. Now I spend most days teaching others to paint but I can't create anything of my own.

Did you have some sort of accident?

Not exactly, he said. But, let's hear about you. What do you do?

I work in a library right now but I hope to open my own bookstore someday. I'm curious about your painting, though. I hate to pry but I'd like to know why you can't paint.

It's going to sound odd but I have a bit of a millipede problem.

I'm still not sure what you mean.

He took a bite of toast and scratched his head. She was a curious woman. For a while, the pair remained silent. He watched as she continued munching on the lock of hair. If she hadn't been so interesting to look at, she would've resembled a lost goat.

The millipedes, he gestured toward the kitchen window. *Just have a look at my garden and you'll know what I mean. It's all gone. Most of it was eaten away long ago. I can't seem to get rid of them.*

The vegetable garden in the back?

Yes.

She pulled the saturated hair from her mouth and stood. A seeping rain had drenched the yard and what was left of the vegetation now drooped sadly with the weight of bad weather. She seemed perplexed as she eyed the garden. He could tell by the way she pressed her lips together and dug at her collarbone until the skin had turned pink.

I can't see anything from all the way over here. So, you have millipedes in the garden and what? How do they keep you from painting?

It doesn't matter, he said. *I shouldn't have mentioned it. It's a silly topic for a first date. Let's have more coffee and talk about something else.*

No, I want to know about the millipedes. Are they large?

Some of them.

They bother you?

They do. It's not the fact that they've eaten most of my garden. It's that they are very noisy. I used to do my painting at night and I find it almost impossible to do it during the day. Now, I teach most days and then sleep. At night, I wake and listen to their noise.

I didn't know millipedes made noise.

I didn't either. At first, it was nothing but a low rumbling sound – like a truck driving down some faraway street. I could still paint, then. If I closed the windows I could barely hear them. But then, a few weeks later, they began to make an entirely different sort of sound.

What sort of sound?

They began to speak.

English?

No. I'm not sure what sort of language it is. I brought a friend over. He's traveled a lot and he knows Italian and French. I know nothing of languages so I figured it could be one of those.

Did he figure it out?

No. He merely concluded that he had heard the language somewhere before but wasn't sure what language it was or what the words might mean.

Couldn't you just look it up somewhere?

I could but I can't hear the words clearly. They either speak too fast or too low. I tried opening the window to see if I could hear better but it didn't help.

Well, perhaps you could make more coffee and I could stay late. I'll see if I can make out the words. I know a bit of Spanish.

I don't think it's Spanish.

That's alright. I can still try, can't I?

He nodded. The pair waited until the sun had begun to set. He prepared a light dinner of fried potatoes and leftover fish. They barely looked at each other as they ate. He didn't like the way her face looked in the dim glow of dusk. Shadows settled beneath her cheeks and made her look older than she was. Her hair – flaxen curls which he first noticed in the produce department, had become frightening and unkempt as night crept into the little house. As he spooned the last bit of fish into his mouth, a familiar hum emanated from the vegetable garden.

Is the window closed?

Yes, she replied.

Could you open it? We might be able to hear them better.

She placed her napkin into her plate and made her way toward the window. She stood there for a moment and contemplated the immense darkness swathed over the garden.

Open the window, he repeated.

She pushed the window open with her small hand. The distant hum became frantic chatter. He sat back in his chair and listened. Foreign syllables and conversations danced in the night. He watched as she stuck her head out the window and then brought her hands to her face. She pressed them against her mouth. A painful, gurgling wail emerged from her thin frame and she sunk down to the floor – fell to her knees in a head with her hands desperately tearing at her face. He breathed deeply as the grotesque choking sound bubbling from her chest continued, solely punctuated by the sharp words of an unknown tongue.

13

Acres of Outback
Louise Kaestner

Gravity drew the first colossal bubble of saline to carve a path through the layer of grime that masked the skin of a delicately boned face. A pink tongue escaped the tiny the lips to sample the flavour of her pain. Surely this is what the ocean tasted like, she thought. Squeezing Green Elephant and burying her face in its worn, terry cloth material, she released a deluge of suppressed sobs from between squeezed eyelids. Darkness enveloped the malnourished frame in a comforting embrace as silent shudders racked her body for fear of disturbing Uncle & Mum in the room next door.

After a time, the tremors ceased & the cleansing flood had run its course. Mother Moon was contemplating her as her eyes opened to stare back. Sister Stars twinkled in greeting through the uncovered window of the room. Smiling, eyelids fluttered closed and a dreamless sleep engulfed Winnie.

Light poured through the thin skin covering her eyes, heralding a new beginning to what already felt like an old day. Lids popped open to witness a solid sheet of sunlight firmly pressed against her body. Relishing the warmth of Father Sun, she lay unmoving, allowing to heal her wounded soul.

The sound of her name being called repeatedly from the kitchen penetrated through her reverie. Still dressed from the evening before, she changed only her knickers. Picking the dirty pair up with haste, she raced through the kitchen, ignoring Mum's glare, to deposit them in the laundry basket.

Returning to the now empty kitchen she seated herself in front of a cracked brown bowl, brimming with rice bubbles, drowned in sugar and dribbled with milk. Pulling a face, she devoured every morsel. Mealtimes, of dubious nutritional value, were unpredictable. Repeated attempts at communicating to Mum about the Healthy Eating Pyramid had resulted in multiple fat lips, amongst other punishments.

"Getting some sticks from Aunty. Clean up after yourself. Laundry needs to be done. Don't wake Uncle." The shrill voice of Mum perforated thin walls of their State Housing accommodation.

Sitting cross-legged 3 feet in front of the television Winnie switched it on, volume barely audible, to wait for the washing machine cycle to finish. Pre-Christmas cartoon films had invaded her favourite cartoon time-slots. Sighing, she flicked impatiently through the limited selection of channels. Settling on yet another remake of The Grinch she became absorbed in the storyline.

Angry yelling & an insistent buzzing from the laundry, filtered through Winnies TV stoned mind. Adrenaline flooded through her guts at the sound of Uncles angry voice. Standing up too quickly, the inside of her head squeezed at her vision until nothing, but a black fuzz clouded it. Hands flew sideways in an effort to recapture her balance. Succeeding, she breathed deeply, and vision cleared. She raced towards the laundry in a belated effort to silence the machine.

The fist of a man, trained in boxing, caught her in the sternum as she flew into the short hallway. Reeling backwards into the lounge faster than she left it, the side of the brown pseudo leather couch, halted her trajectory. Struggling to recapture her stolen breath without releasing a sound was a feat she had become adept in ever since Uncle had moved in.

Uncle had come to live with Mum, Little Brother and herself, 4 years previously. Mum promised Little Brother & Winnie that he was going to look after them all very well. Reflecting back, she wasn't sure if Mum had knowingly lied or not known about Uncle & his ways.

Rough knuckles gouged with accelerated impact into the joint that connected the mandible to her skull. A deafening crack echoed between her ears. The lower jaw was displaced 5 millimetres from the upper. Blood filled her mouth as she swallowed the torrent over and over in an effort to not choke on it.

Chaos had pursued Uncle with his appearance. A month after taking his place at the head of the family, was the night that Winnie had spied the cruel lady driving. A creature that she had tried so hard to forget, had been flying next to car. It's elongated arms, which had more hinges than a humans, seemed to be reaching into the lady's chest and tearing holes in her essence. The mouth was eating the lady's ear without ingesting. It's tongues were weaving vulgar patterns inside her skull.

Impact with the force of a launched torpedo to Winnies unprotected midsection, folded her up as if she was a piece of origami paper. Air was expelled from her mouth, propelling blood onto Uncles foot. Darkness clouded his features from within. A black cloud, deeper than the colour of her skin, penetrated outward through the bloodshot eyes. For an instant, she thought she saw tongues moving through his head.

Little Brother had passed on to heaven 6 months after she had witnessed the cruel lady. The 4 of them had been sleeping in bed together. Awaking suddenly after a terrible nightmare where Uncles hands had been wrapped around her throat, she had sought Little Brother to see if he had shared it. Sharing dreams and nightmares was a common bond that had served to increase stability in a time where Mum had none. Little Brother was already awake, staring at the ceiling, with a look of peace on his face. Speaking to him, receiving no response, she had started to shake him. When his limp body refused to move of his own accord, she had started to yell. Mum had woken up, angry at first, then she too started to shake Little Brother. Uncle had simply slipped out of bed, taken the car keys & driven off.

Face looming, inches from hers, Uncles mouth was moving, yet all she could hear was the rushing of blood in her own body. "I'm sorry Uncle. Please, I forgot. I'm sorry." The words she had spoken seemed to have no effect on the ever-increasing void that seemed to be unfolding out of Uncles head. The heel of his palm smashed into her teeth, wrenching them loose to float in the ocean of blood that had filled her mouth. The Grinch seemed to grin viciously from his face as she lost consciousness.

The sound of tyres screeching gained purchase in her psyche. Burnt rubber filled her nostrils. Sharp pebbles on uneven ground penetrated through thin clothes rendering it impossible for her to stay asleep a moment longer. Sitting up, she opened her eyes & looked towards the rapidly receding tail-lights of Uncles unregistered FJ Holden station wagon. Moments later the unnaturally thick night had swallowed them. A full Mother Moon & Sister Stars were the now only source of illumination.

The surroundings gained a muffled clarity to her mind. Casting a quick glance around her surroundings, Ayers Rock was the only landmark that she recognised. Uncle had followed through on the repeated threat of a solitary enforced walk- about. Unable to recall the incident leading up to this punishment, she stood up.

A movement to her left attracted her attention. A dingo, seat & licking a paw, ceased its activity and looked at her with a quiet knowing. Behind the dingo, was a tear in the steel fence surrounding the national monument. A faded red piece of plastic tape had been tied around a link, to mark where the entrance.

When she had finished dusting herself off, she looked up to see that the dingo had stood up and was now staring at her with an unblinking gaze. The light of Mother Moon was reflected by those abnormally un-canine eyes. Confident of her undivided consideration, a piercing glance seemed to transmit a non-verbal command to follow. Satisfied that Winnie had received the message, it turned around and slipped through the now larger rend in the fence.

Feeling slightly guilty for disobeying Uncle, she decided to follow the dingo. The toes of one foot fetched up against something soft and familiar. Looking down, her Green Elephant was staring back, imploring her not to abandon him, as Uncle had her. Scooping him up gently, she positioned him on her hip, exactly as Mum used to with Little Brother.

The fence seemed to breathe open at her approach, allowing her to pass through unhindered. Once through the fence she could see the dingo standing, body faced towards the Rock, yet looking over its shoulder at her, commanding her to follow. Without giving her time to think, it struck a brisk pace, her feet answering the silent summons.
Following behind the dingo, she would occasionally shift Green Elephant from one hip to the other. Placing her feet where she had seen the dingo place its paws, she realised that the path was unnaturally well worn for the area of Uluru that it was located in. The observation faded from thought as her eyes spotted a moonbeam dancing just above the ground, ahead of her knees. It rose in the air until it was nose height. Turning into a finger, it placed itself upon her nose & gained in consistency until the pressure she felt through the tip had become so insistent that she stopped.

2 hikers backpacks lay directly in her way, with no trace of the owners or where they had walked off to. Overcome with an intuitive knowing, she propped Green Elephant against the packs of the hikers. A feeling of external approval, as if from Little Brother, caressed her in a comforting hug.

Withdrawing her hand from Green Elephant, she noticed light emanating from within. Gasping in delight, she directed her gaze upwards to ascertain if Mother Moon was the instigator. The magnitude and angle of Mother Moon could not account for the brilliance pouring out of her finger. The bones underneath the midnight black skin were moving against each other. The figures underneath the skin became clearer the longer she looked. Each shape seemed to have a twin that was moving in the opposite direction. Circles & triangles, with kissing bums, were the 2 main shapes building the framework of her hand that were becoming ever more discernible. The terms that her year 3 mind were using to relate the information to her conscious mind seemed inadequate. The 2-dimensional terms did an injustice to the 3-dimensional shapes.

Suddenly she noticed the moonbeams finger, insistently beckoning her to follow. Acquiescing to the wordless invitation, all thought of the shapes she had seen fled to be replaced by a curiosity and eagerness she had not felt since before the arrival of Uncle. Gaining momentum up an ever-increasing incline she climbed effortlessly until arriving at the crest.

A square shaped vertical pool of water, absorbing rather than reflect the moon, was standing before her in strict defiance of the laws of gravity. Walking around this liquid monolith in an attempt to asses it's structure, it seemed to be a continuous square with no edge.
Peering doggedly into the clear depths for her reflection, that should have been peering doggedly back out, she decided to sit down. Searching for a comfortable seat, she observed that the ground had utterly vanished. Unphased by the latest anomaly, she lowered herself to the air and folded her legs. Staring into the pond, she waited.

In the distant depths a miniscule blue light appeared, gradually becoming larger. Colours were the first distinguishable feature of the growing image. A gradient that followed the rules of the rainbow purple at the crown, indigo, light blue, green, gold, orange, & red at the core. From the core to the base it sparkled a continuum of outback red, light brown to the deep brown of Ayers Rock itself.

Hues of emotion rumbled throughout Winnies body as her energy, heart and finally eyes recognised the form that was peering out at her from the other side. Standing up, both arms reached out until the palms were resting lightly on the non-reflective surface. The vision of Little Brother that was facing her echoed her action, with the tenderest of smiles adorning his heavenly visage.

It registered in the back of her mind, that this was what he would have looked like, had his life not been cut short. 'Na, Big Sis. My soul was freed of a body that was becoming sick. Uncle did me a favour. You'll see.' Came the thought in his voice, that had never quite grasped the skill of speaking at the age of 3.

'You're an angel!' As the surprised reply ejected from her mind, she realised that her mouth had not moved. 'What is happening? Where am I?'

The smile she witnessed became broader. The gap had been closed between them rapidly so that his body of rainbow shapes seemed to be flush against the interior boundary. Flashes of white lightening seemed to fluctuate across the edges of the rotating polygons where they intersected with liquid. 6 main shapes, some unnameable to her, formed his skinless being.

The thought that was forming in his head had an image that was perceivable to her. Spiralled like a shell, it kept growing until the outer edge aimed for her own head. The summer green tip speared forth towards her, unravelling itself behind the tip. Entering her head, it spiralled into itself until what was once the outer edge, was the core.

'I can come no further for now. You meet me here if you wish.' Whispered the thought that she had moments before observed in its formation and passing.

Accepting the invitation, arms spreading out to either side, echoing Little Brothers, she pressed her body against the barrier. Contact where her shapes intersected with her twin's rendered an energetic feeling of electricity that radiated beyond the boundaries of where the body ended. Peripheral vision observed shards of sentient sparks

79

projecting forth from fingers to eternity. Following one spark with her mind, it continued outwards into space until fusing with an emphasized pulse of light into the Delta Crucis.

It occurred to her, that she couldn't see Little Brother, the square pond or the stars anymore though she could still feel his energy, more strongly than she ever had before. In answer to her unuttered query, 'I'm with you now.'

'How?'

'Your soul knows the answer.' Came the gentle thought.

Somewhere within the centre of her being, an agreement vibrated the answer to her questing mind. It's an answer that is too soulfully profound to be captured by human words or thought processes. It's an answer that is known by the quester. A mere reader may only be introduced to the concept that is the framework leading to the answer, which Winnie seemed to grasp at once in its entirety and then let go of it completely.

A benign, loving repulsion had ignited between the 2 soul bodies. Little Brother was languidly rotating clockwise to Winnies counter-clockwise. The speed of rotation was accelerating to a dizzying pace. For a time Winnie no longer existed separately to her sibling.

Nameless worries dribbled to the forefront of her consciousness to create a sense of unexplainable urgency. When thoughts had gained momentum becoming feelings, they threw her spirit backwards & away from Little Brother. Feeling herself fall from a great height, her essence descended earthwards until she stopped bare millimetres above the deep red earth of Uluru.

Dread stole over her childlike spirit to render a vapid grey the once glorious hues of the rainbow that had fully infused her shapes. Searching for any sign of the Green Elephant and finding none, she lifted her gaze towards the gap in the fence. In the distance, there seemed to be an awful lot of red & blue swirling lights carving a signal through the midday sun. Uncle must be worried about me, she thought.

'Big Sis, there is something you need to see. I will be waiting for you.' Whispered Little Brother in a parting thought to her over-thinking mind.

Needing no encouragement, she tried to run. It was like running through the worst double-g patch ever. Slowing down seemed to make the pain lessen and distance was covered quicker. Nearing the fence, she saw that there was no tear, nor red piece of plastic tape. There never had been. Shock and understanding suffused her essence as she realised a truth of the situation.

Blonde streaked hair framed a misshapen, lumpy, fly infested head. Caring hands tugged the remainder of an emergency blanket to remove the horrifying vision from view. Green Elephant lay 1 metre away from the foot of the covering. Looking up, she saw Uncle sitting in the back an unmarked police car. A sergeant was reading Uncle the Miranda Caution.

Watching the spectacle unfold she remembered it was at this very same location 4 years and 6 months previously, 2 other bodies had been found. The cruel lady had set ablaze in a jealous rage the semi of a cross country truck driver, ending his life & that of his passenger. Turning around she shimmered in surprise. The couple she had just been thinking about, Little Brother in-between, were standing before her. Compassion permeated the expressions of polygon filled unclothed bodies. There was no vulgarity about seeing their true essence thus.

Little Brother extended a hand towards hers to grasp the hand that was mirroring the oncoming movement. Sparks flew & lightening capered throughout her cleansed essence as she fused first with that of Little Brother. The new consciousness of Bli gravitated towards that of GeoRa. Without hesitation the 2 spheres of twins adjusted their rotational axis to a 90-degree offset against each other.

Communication between the spheres was faster than any flesh and skull bound human mind could ever have imagined. Past, present and future of her individual consciousness, of Bli and of BliGra was made known in the passing of a rainbow finger of knowledge. It sewed the 4 individuals & the consciousness of the fused twins together, like a needle & thread. Another new beginning.

Never the end.

14

Morocco Loco
Valery Oisteanu

Women of Morocco

Invisible phantomatic burkas with eyes
Eyebrows like bird's dark wings
Scarf-clad Berber women busy with children
At Riads, smiles of French-educated women-managers
And a team of female servants, appropriate outfits
At Café Tivoli in Fez a singer with "insect-like-eyelashes"
You want a camel burger and a Coke?
Sympatico waitresses laugh in downtown Medina
So many jewelry stores laden with antiques
Artisanal ethnic stores run by women, rugs, pottery
Street figures in hijabs seated on donkeys
Mouths twisted by suppressed endless despair
Country girls with big feet grinding Argan nuts into oil
Full-burka mamas in bazars selling useless souvenirs
Running away angry from the photo-obsessed tourists
Men in cafés, watching the alley's female shadows
Morning drive-by, the river girls washing their scarfs
Harvesting olives in the withered fields
Cooking, taking the shape of a Tagine pot
Sad songs of dead daughters, sisters, lovers
Brides at 13 in photos, sitting beside an old man
Where are those that pray out of sight
The lightning rods of the 2011 Arab revolution
 Mysteriously elusive women of Morocco

Riad to riad

Oh! Traveler the full moon blossoms upon you
Lonely tired traveler is the autumnal equinox
Time to slaughter black sheep from the heard
Time to drink the wine with blood in it
Berbers are singing around the fire
Gnaua sounds, clackety clacks
The songs are loud, trance inducing
At the border of nothingness
Among the shape shifting dunes
The traveler builds a shelter
Out of branches and blankets
Weary camel drivers before crossing
Do not sleep, just trance-ing visions
Walls and gates of the hundreds of Kasbahs
Blind labyrinth alleys, no windows
Smell of burning goat's raises
From the vertical underground pits
Into the souk where masochistic odor
Of a patriarchal medieval subjugation
Hoovers over the mosque, over the women
Over the cities under a bleeding sunset sky
Time for the haunting sin of dreams
Like having102 camels in one's beds
Like losing your shoes in the dessert
The Berbers are sharpening their daggers
While tired traveler arrives to mysterious riad

Children of Kasbah

On the cobblestone streets of Medina
Small dark creatures are shining tourist shoes under the table

Three children on a bicycle driving through the crowds
Children begging, latched to a mother in full burka

Some in school uniforms on winding streets
Other "market-urchins" selling packs of tissues
A bunch of teens scrawl graffiti that reads "Mafioso"
An opposing group writes "Ultras"
With a machine gun underneath labelled "Terrorist"
Victims of neglect create their own demons
Survivor instinct in the maze of Fez and Marrakesh
"The road is closed" the only sentence they know

They will get you lost on purpose for 20 dirhams

So do not offer small coins
On paranoia alleys, children of deceit

Children of poverty with indifferent expressions
Children carrying other children
Carrying round flatbread and Coca Cola Zero
The stink of the dark claustrophobia dissipates
In their sad empty eyes

Goodbye Fez
Goodbye Marrakesh

15

THE DANDYSM OF CAIN
David Nadeau

to kill while singing: realization of the ascesis of an old idea
-Antonin Artaud, *Cahiers du retour à Paris*, August-September 1946

My reflection is based on the work of four blacksmiths of the invisible that can be related to a Cainite current in Romanticism and its historical developments: Gérard de Nerval, Arthur Rimbaud, Antonin Artaud and Denis Vanier. This tradition aims, more or less consciously, at a sublimation of the destructive and self-destructive instincts (desire, anger, revenge...), which are the manifestation of the immense reserve of sulphurous energy evoked by the alchemists under the name of Secret Fire.

An old, lost race,
both accursed and elected,
of ardent demiurgic creators.

"Fire in the center of the earth,
in connection with feminine energies,
I transform selfishness
and,
enormous toil,
I am preparing the upheaval to come."

Currently, the poet has no place in the city and his role is mainly to free himself from the ideological influences (mainly capitalist and Christian) that are dominant there: to unbewitch oneself, in a way. For my part, I can say without exaggerating that I have never been interested in participating in this abelian society. Denis Vanier, an important member in Montréal counter-culture, has also lived most of his life on social assistance, renouncing wage earning to pursue, in poverty, a creative process both political and mystical: "Poetry, he says, is a free gesture with no other goal than to reverse its non-existent social identity. Let's never forget that the poet will be long and inevitably the pariah of any commercial structure. By the way, tomorrow I'm dying from this." (*L'hôtel brûlé*). Society cannot forgive the kind of "fundamental accusations" (Antonin Artaud) that poets suicided by society like Edgar Poe, Gérard de Nerval, Charles Baudelaire and others would carry against it when death stopped them... In the poem "Bénédiction", taken from Les Fleurs du Mal, the latter expresses the mother's feeling of affliction with regard to the vocation of her son, destined to marginality and to general disapproval:

"Ah! would that I had spawned a whole knot of vipers
Rather than to have fed this derisive object!"

"It's I who am Cain, father of the blacksmiths (*Cahiers de Rodez*, April-May 1946)", Antonin Artaud repeats, punctuating his incantatory psalmody with hammer blows struck on an old wooden block. The Talmud tells that Abel sacrifices to Yahweh the most beautiful part of his flock, while his brother, the first revolutionary individualist, first appeases his hunger, before sacrificing some seeds of hemp1, a cursed plant (and, moreover, associated with the star Sirius). He is punished for his impiety, then his face becomes *black as smoke*...

In the time immediately preceding the Flood mentioned in Genesis, the descendants of Cain made such prodigious discoveries in the arts and techniques that they became like gods Until the end of this present "cycle of manifestation", they will work unceasingly to improve the lot of humans crushed by an unjust demiurge. Gérard de Nerval seems to have counted himself among the members of this illustrious lineage ...

In the traditional society, the dual function of the practitioner of black humor (son of Giants), is that of healer and legislator, since he is the one who knows well the old criminal bottom of the human soul and knows how to sublimate it by powerful and effective means:

"All forms of love, of suffering, of madness; he search himself, he exhausts within himself all the poisons, in order to keep only their quintessences. Ineffable torture in which he needs all the faith, all the superhuman strength, where he becomes, among all, the great sick man, the great criminal, the great accursed — and the supreme Scientist — For he attains the unknown!" (Arthur Rimbaud, "Lettre du Voyant").

Denis Vanier, admits that he writes "to not kill, / and thus to expiate / describing this state / sometimes of grace and health" ("Les raisins du lavabo", *Renier son sang*). Metaphysician rocker, he belongs to a body "tattooed by Cain" and whose skin was "pierced by the astronauts of Satan" ("Aux barricades", *L'urine des forêts*).

The Surrealist homeopathy transforms the black earth (Khem,in ancient Egyptian), the fertile peat of the unconscious, nourished by the selfish passions and the dark side of the psyche. This mediation between the visible and the invisible worlds is an operative, concrete way:

"A cart, a plow, a van, a grindstone are more esoteric thanthe Uncreated which is not hiding anywhere"
(Antonin Artaud, *Cahiers du retour à Paris*, December 1946-January 1947).

The superhuman effort to transmit Gnosis in a sensible form that is as much as possible adapted to the degree of moral, intellectual and spiritual degeneration of the present humanity is an unrecognized sacrifice. Nothing is given and everything is always to start again; it is a cyclical, incessant work. I work on a more subtle, imperceptible matter, situated in a potential dimension creator of cultural forms of the Future. In the context of a divorce between the external reality and the dream, from which our technical and commercial civilization suffers, which privileges one to the detriment of the other, I opt definitively for the neglected part of the human mind. The failures of the written language are lodged in the traces left at each stage of a quest for the absolute that only arrives at its approximation. But this approximation itself is creator of eternal realities.

---

1.   As far as I am concerned there may be a key here...

16

Tournament
C. R. Resetarits

> *...because I've noticed that most artists only repeat themselves.*
> —Marcel Duchamp

Marcel gives the west
empty stage save a chair,
to the east empty stage
and a fast spinning wheel.
In between naked Rose
imitation and source
keeps descending the story
by repeating her lines.

Rose smiles secret smiles
as Marcel tips his hat.
Both are servants of lawn ball
willing victims of chess
But always grim knights
flock to possess
maiming her secrets
deboning his hats.

Marcel-and-Rose whimsy
not absurdish per se.
Consider old Alice
how she pondered and fell
fell down that strange well
with the books on the shelves

silly con-curved bookshelves.

Glass, wire, and crinkle
in window displays.
Forks, pins, and skewers
in a city of squares.
One-off found objects
in a readymade box.
3-d sliced meaning
from 4-d nonsense.
A long queue of bachelors
a barely there bride:
all rank and file pieces
all plays of the mind.

*First published as "Shop Window Trumps," *specs* (Fall 2009).

17

The House That Held the Snow.
By Stephen Kirin

Travelling the countryside involved following contours of gently tilted planes bisected by curves and angles under a sky without limits. The snow came late that winter but covered the curves quickly, drifts blown down to the tangent's pattern took weeks to melt back to foundations bedded into the cold enduring clay of deep ditches.

There was one house in a cleft of muddy field, ditch and wood which kept its snow until the next snow; a reminder of a childhood memory shaped by departed family perspective of snow staying meaning more snow coming. This house kept its snow until the next snow whilst all around it returned to green and ochre framing mud. When he left that place he wondered about that house and who maybe in it.

The Earth warmed as the season changed. He voiced a thought,
"Power is real though it defies belief in what can be seen as it's not formed until another notion, like shape or Spring comes into bearing". The shapes in the car that Spring on the A11 acknowledged this as they passed a myriad of solar panels and wind farms playing a game of perspective with energy at the roadside. During daylight both knew the universe stretched all around as well, though obscured by many trajectories and obstacles of the road it was a "given" nevertheless that it was there.

The man in the car preferred to think of the universe in human terms, a retinal imprint or visualisation of a universe within lit up by endless energy, an internal universe also hidden on an everyday basis but there anyway lit up eternally by our own star systems. The person next to him was his star system and she had come to him like he to her via gravitational sling shots to a design not of his hand or a power visible but tangible anyway.

"Do you remember the house that held the snow"?

She turned to him a little on the straight section of road they always noticed that passed where he had once lived. On the right an agricultural feature formed a zig zag, on the left manmade motorway landscaping opened up across a rolling landscape filled with his memories and a road bisecting fields he had once run across. On that occasion he had stripped naked in the dark before sprinting filled with a clamour of sexual frustration that converted into his piston thighs progress, mud between his toes feeling all around him intensely which he now knew was the point.

"Yes" she replied as many journeys passed.

The house that held the snow seemed a long way away by the Summer, as they drove familiar routes in a now parched landscape he thought of it occasionally. He was prone to imagine it as still inside with occasional glimpses of movement from the corner of his eye.

After looking at some Rauschenberg prints of Dante's inferno that he returned to from time to time he fell upon the idea of an upstairs room adjacent to Purgatory with the damned encased in ice...

"Perhaps the upstairs bathroom". He voiced his thoughts to his wife on that years by now normal route.

"No" she replied,

"Definitely the back passage!" with a wink and a laugh the deep ochre harvested dust plains passed. He also thought it could be a frozen house of unfinished memories, the if's, buts and semi realised held in stasis stilled by permafrost. It was funny how the house glimpsed in the snow a few months before still played on his mind.

Summer went at different speeds, the pace of drought baking earth and national speed limit signs passed at a crawl. Calendar marks each week progressed a hard rehabilitation from a fall for an elderly relation, a holiday arrived unplanned. Things passed at speed sometimes blurred became mere anniversaries, the bone mended as the Earth baked.

The view from the fast road opposite the zig zag field boundary towards his childhood landscape may as well have been his childhood. The road to the village quickly glimpsed at 70 miles an hour never changed and sometimes included a view of himself cycling over the small humped railway bridge that marked the turn to what had once been home.

"Do you remember the house that held the snow?" he turned to her whilst speaking, her eyes held him for a moment as she said "Yes".

"We haven't been that way for a while, in a way I don't want to, but in another way I do want to". She turned a little and said there would be more time one day with the voice of someone short of time adding "It probably isn't going anywhere".

The Summer contained a sound that year, an unseen woman's voice punctuated mornings near the relation. Not so much a voice as a series of noises and exclamations that were never explained, starting off birdlike "perhaps like a Bittern" he had once said. By Autumn it was impossible to distinguish from the sounds of birds, crows and gulls; a transmutation from human to bird unseen at its own speed behind a blank façade of another barely glimpsed house.

September came with a change in light, bleached summer colours the harvest and patches of green dappled shade were suddenly spot lit by an angled sun between a frame of longer shadow. Calendar Summer's end included anniversaries both good and sad and the start of Autumn included dates of others. Dates and events passed like long shadows framing a place between seasons, suddenly spot lit like views between cars on the often stationary motorways of that year.

The backend of Summer had included a brief trip to an old house that had featured large in his life, built by his Grandfather it stood like a stubborn edifice against change. The polarity of another house coming to an end after a period of change only made sense in relation to its still look. A decision to move and all that went with it was welcome but kept driver and passenger very busy. Old routes were unfrequented while new ones formed. The route past the house that held the snow had been abbreviated ever since last caught sight of within it's series of road blocks; as one appeared another eased. Among these the relations rehabilitation progressed finally to assisting a move from a cramped environment full of obstacles to an open one full of answers to reduced mobility. Days amongst bisected curves and angles beneath a sky without limits assumed the shape of the everyday again only after the days filled with roadblocks lifted, all bar one which still obscured the house.

A pet leopard gecko had disappeared overnight earlier in the year. The sliding door to the vivarium encouraged open in the dark by the more curious family pet cat. By the time morning came there was no sign of the gecko and theories ranged from him being eaten to just "going". Symbolically geckos sometimes are associated with

reincarnation and regeneration, but does it still count if he's just disappeared and is unseen? She turned to him and summed it up
"He's not doing it for us, it's his journey"
'Of course it is" and so his disappearance turned into one of that Summer's journeys, probably filled with as much scenery and dialogue as any journeys going on elsewhere. One day in September, he came back with no explanation of where he'd been for four months. The only clue was that he was very thirsty and cold. The same cat that freed him had found him and that circle finished there. Of all the explanations, a gecko walking across countryside to the house that held the snow, was the least likely, but cold, thirst and an intangible change amidst the unseen of his journey couldn't be disproved either.

A little time after the gecko returned, the first storm of Autumn coincided with the equinox. A surge of spiralling isobars from the South still dragging warm air up from Iberia. He woke up with a sore throat amidst dreams of a haunted house, sat in the kitchen of this house at 01:30am the doorbell had rung and opening the door, he found a polite but insistent man handing over an envelope of birds that had to be freed. They opened the envelope and black insects emerged moving in all directions. The dream blended well with the gecko anecdote, somehow amidst a slight temperature, the creature they called Bepe had lived with them over Summer in a home of animal design within a home of human design. Somehow dreams of a house held within his head, whilst laying in a house he called home for the time being, led him to thoughts of the house in the snow and the ice he imagined within.

Named storms filled the North Atlantic with narrower and narrower isobars; fingerprints of wind on Summer's neck. Summer had been shaken off by October, but the ever present motorways of the year continued, as did the road blocks, not only near the house, but extending throughout the months. Truncated routes and diversions to, away from and beyond things. The route to work that went past the house, was normally blocked by a ragged hole and luminous striped plastic barriers, they tried to go that way occasionally, but always regretted it. The road was quiet and inconvenience always felt personal, motorway blocks just illustrated collective impotence. A counter weight to this was illustrated on a stopover at the Devil's Punchbowl, in between work appointments and on the way to the frail relation. The old A3 had been rerouted away from the beauty spot and sent underground, leaving nature to cover it. 200 years of moving past the Punchbowl converted into staying at the Punchbowl with stillness saturating the views. Human storms isobars had let their grip loosen after 200 years.

"It's like the grip of us on time diminishing" he said, as she picked herself up after a slight tumble descending Gallows Hill,

"It certainly feels slippery" she replied.

At the cleft of gently tilted planes bisected by curves and angles, stood the house in the snow. On a route superseded by workmen erecting barrier after barrier, matched by other routes and traffic jams; obscuring it's place in the cleft, amidst the snow that did not go, it held it's place. Roads and maps change. His mind returned to an Autumn visit between things to the Devil's Punchbowl which had proved this beyond doubt. Traffic taken away from the old A3 had left space for stress to thaw in that beautiful place and sounds to magnify in synchronicity with the air's amplification. An upturned bell came to mind in place of a covered pot.

And now, as the early Winter snow fell again after months of traffic jams and diversions in heat, dust and obscurity, as work location neared a change and home plans so long coloured by shifting tones of need reached a finality. The longer route to work through the tilted plains under the limitless sky was the route open that day amidst the early snow. The house only seen in snow, still in snow, but altered from before placed among more browns, tans and mossy greens, even umbers and a dash of viridian on some contours. They slowed on the corner that offered a glimpse of the house, a precaution on an icy day that afforded a quick look at detail. Clearly there was a set of footprints heading away from the house in slush that was mismatched with the frozen landscape everywhere else. They passed just in time to register that the house no longer held the snow.

18

4 Pieces
Julian Semilian

Transgender Organ Grinder

I

Call me a stunning redhead, this shift. Here I am, this shift, reclaiming my charge, ensconced in oneiric osmosis with my sister Amaryllis. My sister the carnivorous Amaryllis. Watch me re-assembling my formulations, watch my carnivorous dream assemblage my sister Amaryllis embroiders me in. I am a shimmering weft of disobedient vatic intimations, having mastered in a concert of past shifts, notably as a prize in the Babylonian lottery, the tenuous task of oneiric mirroring by scent.

I have been assigned, this shift, with the task of scenting the odor of nightmares so as to metabolize them before they coagulated into the casual quotidian. Having only recently emerged from a self imposed exile to a corporate asylum for the psychically restrained, the exuberantly confined, I was still somewhat thwarted in my insurgencies by the last of a frightwork of prohibitions. Yes, a certain phantasmical restrictedness still circumscribing my personal balletics that osmosis with Amaryllis was dissolving, anthracite frightwork I acquired from the shift in this asylum, still gasping from the fumes of thwarting, this asylum honing wardens of restraint by propitiation, genuflection to mandalas of inevitability, shunting public ridicule on a shrine of restraint.

Who am I this shift? Descend into my bowels and you'll find me not; nor will you find him I consumed, him of whom I will speak; him of whom I still wish to speak; who am I this shift? am I no more than my fitting form of imponderable emerald clarinets? Is my shimmering weft of disobedient vatic intimations, of impertinent events, the purpose of That which gave me shift? Am I peerlessly loomed with the fulgurant fingers of the Imponderable? I've peered for purposeless aeons into notions of my own essential peerlessness.

But to my purpose, this shift, prevention of a coagulating nightmare. It seems that a certain Gordo had frozen his lovely consort Andrea in the hose of submission, in the act of genuflecting in a propitiatory prie-dieux, before his posturing on a shrine to his priapic preoccupations.

Gordo was no more than an economic actor, his inner formulations were well integrated in the dogma of the feeding frenzy, yes, his inner formulations were the mandatory remedies of the day, the pale fire of pre-established September twilights was blinding to him, he was no more than a mere link in a frightwork of internetting fuhrers of an industry of amnesia engendering incentives, a corporate Romeo impaled by the perpetual beckoning spin of a bewitching mannequin, grafted as motivational effigy before the forced march of the common activity.

Yes, Gordo had earned his personal post on the malady scale by grafting pre-established September twilights on Andrea's disciplinary hose, forcing her formulations to flounder in a whirling spin of abstracted lemurs, forcing her to peer incessantly into cross-eyed civets of self-contempt.

Yes, his praxis was to neutralize you by forcing you to peer into the frightwork mirror of his pre-animated definitives, to suction you into the zone of amnesia his dogmatic psychic manipulations occupied; he aspired to a posture as a fuhrer in factories for honing the propitiation techniques of the populace, hierophant of amnesia engendering incentives. To obscure this deformity he sprayed himself in azure tornado veneers and cast himself as a turbulent drama, causing his lovely consort Andrea to secrete an amber tarantula butter, but an amber from which all insurgent thought was removed, from which the Imponderable was pampered into quartered marmalade. Of this she herself could not discern.

II

Here I am riveted to my stunning aspect. Oh, my fitting form of emerald clarinets! Iridescent weft of disobedient vatic intimations! Oh my lucifer hose, obsidian shimmering within the deeper obsidian, incandescent eruptions of the vertiginous balm! Oh, the ballet of my fulgurant fingers!

I was where I no longer needed to consume myself for consuming the one who entranced me, the one I secured to my own persona, the one I left like a broken clavichord in the corner, the one I have a wish to speak of, the one I had said yes to. Yes, the one I consumed, the one I still have a wish to speak of.

Though his predilection was mantled in the imaginal vestments of a Venice Renaissance, he left the door open for an even grander solar mystery. "As I have transcended a life of economic principles", he purled, "my gesticulating is unimpeded by the mere mores of the teutonic pedagogues of utility." He made me peer into the collection of kaleidoscopes he kept, factoried of shattered chambers of obsession, manufactured of vaguely melted maternal restraints.

Yes, his telos was a method he honed by hurling intuitional boomerangs into a unfriendly nest of absolute iguanas, through which he had transcended the institution of umbilical shackles, factory of interpretational restraints, restraints in service of the pervasive shackling of the exuberant. He hissed at ideas of fixation, spat in the face of libido arrest, painted me freely in hierophant hose, an attire which in his mirrors I adored.

He spun hypothetical cultures through hymns he intoned in praise of one's multiple spin of despised inclinations smoldering at one's core, which he perceived as the true anthracite of tumbling into sudden resorts of vatic cormorants — cormorants I might add he summoned at will — and maintained, as in a hatchery, as in a nest of restless water moccasins he'd grafted to a private sector of his obsessional ambiguity, an ululating coterie of impertinent events.

He had reduced the renaissance to an ageless mental precipitate, which he spat at his shivering adversaries, along with a general purview of the crusades, causing them to become unhinged and hurl crudely digested chunks, lingering shards of reinforced dogmas regarding the dilemma of the brooding formulations of their shifty eyed god, always plotting floods in the corner, always calculating the quantity of mercy on demeaning scales, always chewing on the forehooves of demons. This shifty eyed dog they worshipped, before the altar of quartered exuberancies, before mandalas of concrete inevitabilities, shifty eyed dog always organizing the quartering of chimeras in the corner. "I have never craved his rusty validation", he frightened them. "My formulations are an of emerald of my own redeeming. For the deviation of the sun", he touted as they cowered, "is a nightmare of circles, not the panning for gold in ostracized forests, not the beseeching of the frightwork glittering of nightmare littorals, littorals I have long been assured of."

He called me his mountain fountain, his eerie valkyrie, and promised to initiate me into his praxis of how to turn this spin of despised inclinations smoldering at my core into a full vatic opera featuring me as the murderous fravarti leading the viper retinue, baritone soprano to be worshipped in emerald clarinets by agitated crowds across the peanut galaxy. "The cruel solar flare, the day's odious conspiracy against those who dream", he declaimed as he enraptured me, and I said yes, yes, I said yes and I let him capture me in the fulguration of his firebrand fingers and leaped aimlessly to his vertiginous verb flamenco.

And yet the blinding glimmer of my emerald clarinets was like quicksand to him, was the shock of a sudden nest of water moccasins (which, blinded, he rendered as vatic cormorants.) "Chant me in your intimate anthems", he pleaded. "Make me the shadow of your peerless solar clarinets."

And I said yes, and condensed the precipitate of his fierce essence in my own persona, secured his ululating coterie of disobedient events inside my own intriguing formulations; his gesticulating, so entrancing to me, — irregular balletics I so craved as my own as I craved the insurgency of his clairvoyance to spring from my chords, not his — unimpeded as it was by the mores of the teutonic pedagogues of utility, this gesticulating so entrancing to me, and I undressed him of it and embroidered it to my own core.

Yes, I said yes, and I swallowed it slowly till I felt it shifting inside me as my very own persona, as my ballet of disobedient iguanas, till it became my own brand of irregular balletics.

Yes, you could say I secured him with the quicksand glimmer of my emerald clarinets which he adored, yes, you could say I gave voice to the frantic chorus of smoldering assassins at my core, assassins *he* released, assassins whose intriguing formulations I followed, followed *his* intriguing formulations, yes, and yet it paralyzed me to know he became a broken clavichord in the corner. "I will make myself the subject of ridicule", I declaimed, craving to inflict retribution on myself, "denounce myself before a scornful crowd."

But the paralysis lingered, and, contrary to my nature, condemned myself to a corporate asylum for the chimerically confined; there, to spite myself, I charged my murderous fravarti armada smoldering at my core with the mission to frighten the male populace by tricking it to peer into suddenly ambiguous mirrors; and there I multiplied myself in distress by absconding trans-temporally with protesting pre-Baroque Venetian baronets, yes the weather was right for trans-temporal travel, for protesting pre-Baroque Venetian baronets, entranced by the murderous glimmer of my emerald clarinets, at the precise moment of the ecstatic swoon, I, priapic fravarti in murderous emerald clarinets, and committed sortilege by embalming them live inside my own brand of mandala made living by their supine lowings of blinded male Juliets — here I must pause to point at shattered fragments of crusades prematurely abandoned, spontaneous acts of barbaric intrusions, erratic scrawlings of corroded bits of screaming baronets, of these I drew my new clarinets, more fierce, of these bubbled the essence of my new balletics — framed in diorama formulations of an intriguing crocodile amber, then, utmost of disobedience, intrigued the populace to insurgency by trading them, the baronet mandalas, for tickets at the Babylonian lottery.

I repelled general attacks of invasive sulphur lapping at my core by fanning myself with the delectable feather of Treason I honed when I was first initiated, do you recall? as a prize in the Babylonian lottery. That, the lottery, long before their wardens of genuflection imposed restraint by propitiation under that barbed frightwork of their shifty eyed dog they worship, always spitting his brooding formulations in the corner, always calculating the quantity of mercy on his contemptuous scales, always organizing the quartering of chimeras in the corner. Yes, not one to celebrate treaties too long, always seeking palaces ablaze with the Imponderable, I left in my place the lure of a bewitching mannequin to keep the consensus alive.

(Here I divagate to declare, I view Treason and Adoring equally, enmeshed as I am in my frightwork of blinded tarantulas, loomed with the fulgurant fingers of the Imponderable, and I balance between one and the other like the swift incandescence of a midnight fawn.)

III

So, here I am riveted to my stunning aspect. Here I am, the baritone ballerina mantled in the imaginal vestments of a Renaissance Venice. Here I spit in the face of libido arrest, here I paint myself freely in hierophant hose, an attire which in my mirrors I adore. Let my shimmering weft of disobedient vatic intimations, of impertinent events, be the purpose of That which gave me shift. I've peered for purposeless aeons into notions of my own essential peerlessness. Now let me be peerlessly loomed with the fulgurant fingers of the amber Imponderable!

IV

As I mentioned, Gordo's modus was to neutralize you by forcing you to peer into the frightwork mirror of his pre-animated definitives, to suction you into the zone of amnesia his dogmatic psychic manipulations occupied.

I could have, of course, conducted his hibernating vipers to re-arrange his definitives by suddenly intoning off key, caused the canned hurricane of his crocodiles to blow without aim; but I was afraid the prolonged nightmare diet he had placed his crocodiles on might have caused his amnesia to burst out of proportion and thus season Andrea prematurely; it wasn't my intention to smuggle her out as a burning Christian.

In oneiric osmosis with Amaryllis I devised the following ploy: through the praxis of the incantatory, to reassign the frightwork reticulation of his amnesia by shunting it to fresh venations which would cause him to act convulsively, in the manner prescribed by the poets, to lure his longings to leak out of the zone of pervasive amnesia his dogmatic psychic manipulations occupied, to trick his assemblage into rendering the shimmering yawn of Amaryllis in the purple hues of the convent of adoration Andrea had fashioned for him, transcending the entrancing September twilights of his own formulations, thus trespassing the carnivorous zone of Amaryllis while giggling in the grip of his priapic preocccupations, as though to barter them for the convulsive contraband he had secretly striven for.

"This intoning in reverse of enchanting quicksand", I chanted, "this whirl of lucifer words I flutter in your corneas, this frightwork chorus of assassins at my core, this nest of water moccasins I've now secured you in, yes, you, you, in whose corneas I now flutter, this weft of emerald clarinets you've secretly wished me to secure you in, a sacrificial offering you've craved to make of your weft of multiple despised inclinations you've couched in amnesia, sacrificial offerings to my full vatic opera with me as your murderous fravarti, your corneas, yes, your corneas melting in sacrificial offering to this frightwork chorus of emerald assassins at my core, blinded tarantulas in the employ of tyrannical prophecies, yes, my clarinets, blinded tarantulas in the employ of tyrannical prophecies, this vatic opera you now perceive as the flutter of my obsidian words, weft of emerald clarinets to secure you in, nest of water moccasins you've wished to be secured in in sacrificial offering, and you said yes, yes, my emerald obsidian corneas, witnesses to your soft dying..."

I needed to chant no longer: he felt himself craving to mimick the forced morphallaxis of phantoms. "I have always longed to balance on the soft shoulders of glow-worms", he giggled convulsively as he flung his frame into Amaryllis's yawn and diaphanously metamorphosed into the protoplasmic jet of her lavender metabolical rage.

I peered at Andrea. Her hose of submission had suddenly transmuted into the alabaster balletics of re-released vatic iguanas! Her formulations no longer intoning hymns to the civets of self contempt. "I will order statues to your frightworks to be chiseled in Emerald Imponderable", she shouted and leaped. She was suddenly entrancing, like perusing into peerless solar clarinets. Their luminous spill made me rash and I shot out my fulgurant fingers — o the ballet of my fulgurant fingers! I, priapic fravarti, riveted as I was to their luminous spill! Architecture of peerless soprano celestinas!

No, I was not about to examine the translucence of limbs under the moral microscope, as momentary self entrancement was my purpose, come what may...

Tango

i don't wish to criticize you, but you are badly tailored: your headlights are inside out and your streetcars splay the stepmother's purple pitch. to tell you the truth, i am undone over the vapors of my circumstance and demean myself with droll anecdotes about your iron negligée. it's not that i'm delighted with this alternative: but my portion is as rigorous as the amorous affairs of a miraculous mandarin. i would have loved to holler at the emperor's hora, instead of the screech of the skylark i found inside the leeks you cooked for me with the screwdriver. but i don't wish to seem like i'm complaining: i have plenty celluloid to protect myself against the mechanism of your succulent and carnivorous sunflower; and from time to time i lose myself inside the splinters of a moldavian rain forest. then i squeeze like a burglar through the silk of the spiders exulted over blue fever belladonna trysts. in fact, once i made very good use of my pneuma to bash my head against the sun, and your violin. the blood flowed through your garters and the dried grapes fetched me boiling coffee full of fairy tales spun inside roosters and bulls. yet in spite of these successes i still cast my dice over bridges overpowered by the erotic quakings of lawns observed from trains trudging though moist dusks during the time that you, do you remember? spent without me in cities where the dawn obsesses over the teeth of poisoned smoke. and i didn't want to leave you alone, or perhaps i couldn't, because you played your violin with the rivers of blood in the books i hadn't yet written. and please forgive me that i chronicle such intimacies but my goal-keeper calling just doesn't suit me. i had dreamed of being your crab apple tree or at least some unfriendly dreadful mustard to lubricate the occult caves of your music. perhaps this discordance was meant to teach us a dance, a crouched tango professed by the palm leaves of compassion which even the trade winds could not bend or separate from your severe and invisible crimson garter. i used a wand of red fog to startle your vaguely turbid water and i was threatened by the queen of the creeping onion shrubs, who, from way back in the feudal ages milked the cow inside the quicksand. she lit her cigar on the wagon wheel of my involuntary army and stalked me through the days i slept late so as to frighten me with fables of yet unoccupied superhighways and vampires of frail milk who were abandoned by our neighbors' autumns. even so, she lent me tobacco and plates of spider sugar which she hatched under her armpit of silver stolen from her cinder cousins. i was grateful for these gifts which i wore proudly on my furious necktie but i wasn't sucked in by the excessive value you placed on them on the soccer fields in your blood. and as for the places where i wanted to be most: i had to sneak in, like a lithe child of flames, thief of beer and cherries; and when i was there i told you nothing about it, yet hoped that you approved and wouldn't scorn me too severely had you surprised me spitting out my mournful accordion seeds.

cipher violin

my yearnings trained me in spit contests where I won oranges and beer, which I carelessly tossed over the bridges you crossed that afternoon, do you recall? when I squandered sand on your little baby red shoes. You whimpered and gobbled a whole donkey; then, upon awakening, still groggy with disgust, charted for yourself the countenance of a night owl; I easily diagnosed you — true to your disorder, you snorted — and when I got home I bashed my head against the faucets until the pigeons winged away with crimson messages for you. you mimicked miscomprehension, and like a stubborn ballerina of obsidian, had your little baby red shoes messengered to me, belligerently demanding reparation. I shook the sand off impatiently but later shifted my drift and effortlessly dissolved them on a moonless night (my joints intransigently enmeshed in my notorious allure of a blue fever belladonna pitch) then preserved them inside a trade manual I dried in the wind, diligent daily visitor, intent on teaching me the uses of the violin. And he didn't denounce me even though I was lazy — so you vaunt — and my days and years went to waste; and even now the violin is still an amber imponderable to me but when I spit, the wind squeezes through the beckoning of your little baby red shoes, and howls a doleful tune, and everyone rushes out, clapping in unison.

sapphire turtle bride

you were the arch of triumph and your voice still makes my eyes genuflect. i persevered in my determination to lick the salt of our mutual sour cream and i preserved my eyes inside an old dutch tobacco pouch where a few world wars had ignited, smoky willows and all, including the obligatory vacations. i fluttered my lungs and straightened my eyes and afterwards gave my life over to literature and wine; and when i came home i found you completely transformed: you were a foggy bride full of dirty teeth, splinters sticking out through them; and hardly anything was left of the mandolins which i was saving for the times when uncle victor comes to see me and eat the pastrami which you and i bought when we bought the mournful blinding twilight rugs, the ones you adored but two days later forgot at aunt claire's when we went there visiting her; and you swore to me that it is not true that you forgot them there because you didn't adore them anymore (which i believed) but that it had been an accident of forgetfulness which could happen to anyone; and you scolded me very harshly, yes indeed, you were a little too harsh with me that evening when you offended me deeply by calling me a freudian cretin; and you said that's why you treat me so mean because i am so doubtful of myself and so lacking in audacity that i have a need to freudianly analyze everything to feel good about myself, shrouded up as I was in my bedsheets of sun, and then you left with my wallet where i kept my kansas city shoes and my eyes of tobacco ash.

19

Meeting the Rain and the Missing
James Not'in

The rain has been merciful on us this year, not that it wasn't in the previous year, but is one too thankful at the birth of a twin?

The rain came earlier we had enough to time to plant maize thrice, to mark the special harvest, we have gathered each with the best of our produce, there was a pot at the centre of the circle we formed, the village was crowded than the crowning of a king.

It was Lara that stepped first into the centre, she migrated her waist to the tunes that were forbidden but the king loves the beads and the rhythms, it became normal to dance before the kings' speech. Before now, we have witnessed the death of children; death was nice to our village adults that he only makes love with young ones.

The priest said we must appeal the god and search within our city, for one of us have defiled the rules of the gods; not smoking on Sunday. This is a day the gods chose for themselves and smoke disturbs their breathing.

When I was just seven, the rain hasn't stopped at our village for months; farmers were on kneel from sunrise till the sound of mortals call them back to home eat before the rain comes. Then I asked my mother why I was born with no tongue. She failed to satisfy my inquisition, she only said, it is not time.

After Lara had danced and men have thrown corns and millet at her, the king steps down, before now, the king has always been in a place we don't know. We only see him a day after harvest has been equally distributed and most goes to the palace.

More than the crown on the king heads, for the first time, we see him and he is not different from us. We scream and shouted, our noise interest the birds that they abandon chirping and listen to our music. Everywhere was filled with happiness and somewhere the unsatisfied sat drinking palm wine to get them happy because a year like this deserves celebration by being happy.

The king returned to his seat, as his plan to talk was interrupted by some young dancers, they took the entire village square on un-notified. As they dance a lady step out in hijab but she was stamping her legs, I could hear the sounds of her bangles and gold, the Muslim clerics were shaken but the festival continues.

Finally, when the king comes down, the names of the dead had filled the air, our ancestor has returned in cotton sewn together, they fly like birds, vanish into the slight breeze and return in another direction. When I was eight my mother claimed the reason the youth were dying
was that our fathers have forgotten the way home.

The newness that engulfed our village has disrupted the rituals of welcoming them. The circle was filled by young and the feeble, in one of my dreams at the stream, I saw women dancing in the village square, men drumming, the young admitted light to everywhere the village turns. I am trying to wake up now, as this is a remembrance of that dream.

During the times when the rain could not enter our town, we have habitually saved our tears in a cup, sometimes we drank from it or invest them in the only maize that survives the harshness of time on the Kings' farm. We burn the dead, and we save their ashes for later days when we the soil is too weak.

The king could no longer sit behind, he jumped into the circle and there was at first no one else left except him. Lara stepped out into the circle and the dancer joined, the women and the men also joined, I was somewhere at the edge of the forgotten circle, moving in silence.

It was the crown that the king first took off, the beads, we haven't seen him in ages but now before our eyes, he is just a flesh like us. Some said it was the rain that took him away. When I asked my father in one fruitless day at the farm, he said the king was closer to the god, but we determine how the gods react to the king.

On the same farm, my father fell with the last standing tree on the farm; I wish it wasn't that easy to lose a pillar. Like every other body that fell during the years rain was gone, my father ashes was saved in a black earthen pot, and later when the priest said she saw death around the corners of our house, I sprinkled the ashes to scare them off.

Despite the rain that visited us, we nevertheless keep grieve in our heart, so as the king danced, we threw sand at him, some ashes of the dead; this is also a way of welcoming back a missing person. He wasn't disturbed by our reaction to him, at some point, he ate the ashes and we began to feast of the corn that has boiled in the village square.

Before my grandfather died, he had said he only witnesses a festival like this when he was ten years old. I guess I am opportune. The king sweat dripped on the floor and from it, sorghum sprang up, this made us believe the gods are back with us. Our ancestor had gifted the spirit which occupied this land before us sorghum on their resettlement here, them giving it back to us does not mean rejection but a validation of days to come.

We haven't discovered the person that smoked and cleared the path for the return of the gods, but now we merry till morning when the priest reminds us that we need to get that person out of town. The gods are back, so are our fathers, can they still be angry if they are here? I wanted to ask, but I knew it was best to keep the rain.

The dance and eating haven't stopped, the sad ones are now drunk and happy, the king is still dancing unnoticeable in the circle, and then the lady in hijab requested for silence. I knew silence in a time as this is not needed at all, or essential to keep us in this state. Silence envelops the square, and we saw that she had been overridden by our father, her eyes were un-behold able she pointed at the king, the sad people rushed to the side of the lady.

There was silence; the crying baby was faithful to the code of the moment. The interruption of silence was from the king, he requested our attention and it came out clear, he smoked on Sunday. The sad ones said that was right, the lady in hijab left with the wind.

20

Two Poems
Allan Graubard

... for Laurence Weisberg

Soon you will be a poem between the pages of a book
And every futile lovely smile or grimace will dissolve in image in metaphor
You will not taste but we will taste you
Believing that we've met again
On one of those empty streets 3 pm, no one about

The language you envied exalted despised caressed
Will dream your sudden presence
And we will sip our wine wondering whether or not you can hear our thoughts
We will kiss each other in the low lamp light
Singing silently to the silence that surrounds silence

We will sit in the park smoking an empty autumn afternoon
We will emerge from who we were and transpire like great bridges of spume
Left on lunar tides

Somehow the virgin nocturnal will unwrap delicate emeralds
And her hands will blossom patch works of tar
Stiff cracks of blood
Patches of mold on the burning windows where she strips night from her eyes

Soon it will be too late at Bardo thermal
The necklace of bones will strangle viaticum
Later we met at the bar on 6th street
Wind of wind
The ephemeral city

You wore your hollow face
            ... a poem between the pages of a book.

... for Billy Bang, Violinist

There is no turning back now

No definitive exodus to the hinterlands bled dry

The great plectrums of cash that sink out of sight

Untouchable necromantic visions of largess in cuspidors

Latent viaticum in the transient ward

I've had that final comeuppance and woke at the edge of brittle sentiments in a blue room that whirled on oily axels of petrified sugar

The sixteen leap years where I raised my hands to sparkling nomad swallows

The thirty-two juggernauts of mistletoe that burned at dusk on a subway track between 96th and 103rd street

Simple words that I can't forget in the meantime cross vacancies and pull on red licorice socks

They tell me the time on Jupiter while fondling diamonds of Omphalos

Sooner than later you're gone

And all that worry, work, love, anger, frustration, joy, despair, louche stoicism before corrosive injunctions and bestial stomas, filial touches in the concussive light behind the eyelids smoke off until silent empty glances phantom glint with essential chords in B-flat minor

 ...and that's as far as it gets on the planisphere roaring in a sunflower's possum pocket watch, the decal peeling off, deft trumpet scorch marks clinging by their fingernails to heaving rivers of emulsified bark

Listen, listen low and long

There is no turning back now

The hurricane walls have crumbled and the marshes stroke dynastic wolf cairns, turtle egg fabulists, archaic deer with albino muzzles and thin dialectics

Where busty shadows deal green black jack
                              and life on the run runs out

i rot because i'm cut
Judyth Emanuel

Seven Disconnections Tell Me

1

How the light gets in. Cracks enormous threatening break the
walls of my house begins splits jag into a lightning shape
cracking zap. And the foundations subsiding now I thinking big
worry rats burrow through. *Rats!* Or what if a river of blood
bursts? From the cracked. Places. Gush rush down the stairs. Like
The Shining. WELL IT COULD.

       He laughs his jack laugh. Buys plaster. Gobs up the
damage. Done.

2

Get rid of what? The rot. Everything. Lighten the load. Sell E-
bayed destroy *give it away*. Every stuff crap. Really. His insistent
bossy. His prickle voice.

       Go on Go on Go on Go on Chuck It Out. Just do it. What
have you got to lose?

       WELL! A gravy boat missing the matching saucer. My blue
Esky dreams of picnics where. In the botanical gardens tartan rug
spread under a shady tree. Water lapping somewhere. And how
does my small violin become so smashed? Somebody sat on it
keep it anyway sad. And tuck away out of sight a naked man just
a trophy. Him a shiny fake gold. I dust the statue's balding head.
All bald bland stands. Italics carved inscribed burn into his plastic
pedestal *Over 40 And Still Standing*. Unsmiling. Of damaged
goods, superfluous items drag at me the way things do. Get out
my antique shotgun. Give it a wipe. Now dust free disarmed. So, I
cannot shoot myself and put an end to this CUT LIFE.

3

Him away back when. Get him home soon. I swim kill time
wherever public pool. Beach toweled walking home. Hang black
swimsuit on the bathroom door handle. Close the door. Shut the
world out. Shower sings popcorn jello songs tramps like us born
to run. Suds slippery girl-woman. Of rub. Calms my dry skin
open the bathroom door. A black shape sudden swings in. Yikes
help Jesus almost screaming but scream sticks inside throat. Shit
scaring the out of me. This small headless panther. Why a wild
cat pounces. I have no pussy. And I do a panic silly sees my
mouth of open at the one-piece swimsuit swinging wet drips.
What of my fear two seconds shock. Alien bathers. Blow by a
breeze. But. No wind blows in the airless room. Inanimate objects
with a sense of humor wonder about this. The everything very

funny. Scream swim shower suds slip on soap *hilarious*. In some
way. I cut a bit.

4

Why a plenty person, skips, flails arms. Not too crazy.
Today a bit of happy in a flap. For Absolute No Reason. Rolled
around on the bed King sized roll. Shook my legs in the air. Leapt
big leap trampolined to attention. Heard crack. Oops. Bed-base.
Shattered kaput. I crumpled. Knees killed me. What was I. What
was I doing. HERE. Exuberance quitted the go. A still life. Not
good. Bad knees. Expired bed. All cracked up to be.
So much pain. ?#@*%!

5

Today meant me make a mighty effort. Get out of the house. Cut
a rug! At some point the cracked must. Take a vacation should
we. Go. Someplace nice a place can there exist such a
whereabouts location. Where I fit in!
     Like the Country Heart of very far away paddocks. Surprise
yell my yell,
        What's that in the distance?
        Oh My God. It's a horse!
     Just the one. Horse. And the soft gusts. And the branches of
trees lean to the left. I squint bigger at distant wonder. Convince
this a mechanical toy battery-ing to gallop. A hoof cloud in the
shape of. Or a cow skinnier, donkey taller, zebra unstriped.
Maybe paler. A pale horse. Trick of the light.
        Great. I need a light horse.
     Walk the further got us close. A closer look. Damn. Laugh
cracks us. That horse is a dark horse. Of course.

6

Hey love high on a pedestal. Passion cracks open a thing
 imagined. Get me some. Of it now. Nothing as pure as true as
what I imagine. For a while. Him. Oh Christ. What that
imagining? The recipe for perfect love. We have which is. Which
needs clover, bees, a dream. What if bees are few. Then The
Dream Would Do.

7

From the seventeenth floor. We hear a brass band where well
there. Plays brassy things in the street below. *Oh when the saints*
what saints *they go marching in. When the saints.* Oh. This band
marching of. Confuse sounding. Music refuses to keep in time.
Trumpets all over the place. Drumming too soon. Flutes trill at
will. I lean over the balcony. Cannot get a where. The band. Must
be a ghost band. Confident they them ghost bands exist. How for
certain. So unsure after. Never indisputable because of what.
Ghost band hyper invisible. But we really really hear it then and
 then it. Plays a different tune. Speed of tempo. Quicker ooh.
Hurry.
     Life goes on. Life goes on. Life goes on.

Faster. Horn hits whacko wrong notes that's.
Life.
Sudden ambulance siren adds itself to the music noise.
Goes. What if someone injured overdosed heart attacked person
on crack stabbings decapitation old age. *On.* Well wiggle hips us
slow jive music. This. Helps. No matter how badly the band
playing. Music drowns out tragedy. And a cut life. Goes. On.

22

TWO TEXTS FROM 'THE TOWER OF LIBERTY'
Stuart Inman

The Tower of Liberty

Words and images, like the things they represent, are in ruin. The cracks in a wall conjure a wolf or a fox, all that remains of Chateau LaCoste, Sade's home and refuge. Less remains of his most notorious prison, the Bastille, a stain on the memory of Paris and the irony of his gaolers in naming one of the towers, the very one that held Sade, Liberté.

To enclose that most stirring of words in the context of forced domination of one part of the populace by another, to reduce it to a joke, that seems to me the true perversion, not Sade's desires. The Tower of Liberty – is it possible to turn that phrase inside out, return it to its true meaning and declare it a citadel of freedom? Difficult though it may be to enflesh this idea in our state of diffuse unfreedom, it seems at times to emerge from that mist like Caer Sidi, "turning without motion between three elements".

Can the Tower of Liberty be all that refuses to go into the totalitarian equation, everything that denies the supremacy of the market or the vacuous opiate of the media world? But, like Caer Sidi, it must remain a subjective phantom unless we give it the substance of our own flesh and the reality of our desires.

Sade negates the mental prison in his fury and reveals the spiritual sewer of his captors, nor does he spare himself. He reveals the complicity of each of us both in our criminal freedom and as our own jailers. To what extent is our freedom tangled with our simultaneous imprisonment, our innocence and our guilt? I do not have the answers, I only see the tower, a lighthouse of black radiance.

But the simple inversion of the prison tower into a citadel of freedom, a chateau of surrealism, is not enough. An image, more disturbing, more perverse, presents itself. The phallic tower folds and unfolds itself, becomes vaginal, hermaphrodite monolith of flesh and melting stone, forever fucking itself as shrieks of black and white light illuminate or hide a dark, convulsive sea.

The Analogical Frenzy

The analogical frenzy never subsides. Caught in the game of mirrors where a face other than my own looks back at me, the old question "Who am I?" reasserts itself. The notion of the other, the one that is not I, seems inadequate. Rimbaud's maxim that I is *an* other is a little more slippery, a suggestion of other others, a multitude.

Language, which fixes identity in its utilitarian aspect, breaks it apart in the field of analogy, allowing a very different range of connections to take place. It is no longer a matter of unity, for unity smashes the particular in order to create a single identity. The non-dual on the other hand brings the non-identical particulars into an open field of relations. It is here that the principle of analogy reigns.

Analogy names the non-identical resemblance. Therefore, in the natural world we have: stagbeetles, hawkmoths, atlas moths, snapdragons, dragonflies, cobra lilies, starfruits, sunflowers, foxgloves, bee orchid, slipper orchid, lyre-bird, peacock butterfly, tiger's eye, moonstone, moss agate, dandelion, ant-lion, scorpion fish, lawyer's wig, earth-star, ox-eye daisy, oxlip, cowslip, tiger moth, rhinoceros beetle.

The tension of proximity between non-identical elements engenders the spark that allows the authentic voice of the poetic to emerge.

23

Two Poems
Jake Berry

Oracular

"Your sons and daughters will prophesy,
your old men will dream dreams,
your young men will see visions."

So it must be
for as I settle into my dotage
all manner of fiery seraphim
scatter fragmented narratives
and luminous imagery
across the theater in my skull, my heart
and that vast invisible, unnamable chamber between

So it must be
until I cross the Lethe
or drink from the pools of Mnemosyne
and you'll see me no more
except in memories –

and perhaps, dreams

The Art of Vanishing

I sleep
I dream
I carry the deathbed
a little further down the road

The art of vanishing is so easy
we barely notice the effort

The young woman at the plough
throws seed on the ground
and walks away

She spits and the rain comes
We can never recover

from this disaster

But when I turn in my sleep
the myth is reborn
with a new cast of characters

and I notice
the road winds
through a stand of elm
and dove song rises
from its depths

24

Mud Puddle
Eleanor Levine

I'm doing all the right things: dressing up as Dear Leader and eating a box of chocolate for Halloween.

*

The ex does not respond to emailed punk rock pumpkin photos of me and the cat and me and the dog or me dressed as Kim Jong-un, with an expensive green jacket and Dear Leader mask from Amazon.

*

I wonder *why* I'm going to her daughter's birthday with a frozen Trader Joe's pumpkin cheesecake that will melt by the time I get there. Like our relationship, which also melted.

*

In the end, she says, there is a storm brewing, please do not come to our party.

*

She came out to her mother, after 40 years—a month after we "split up."
Was it my personality, so pathetic, that she needed support, openly, from her mom, and that's why she came out? "OK, I'll be a lesbian, and Mom, it's okay, *I really want to be one*, and I'm coming out now, after 40 years, so you can keep me away from psychotic women."
"What do you mean, sweetheart?" her mother asks.
"My ex flies in the clouds, like a turnip in a hurricane."
"You don't like turnips, honey?"

The ex is quiescent.

Doesn't talk or respond to my emails about a short story—the Jersey Devil one, which is timely for Halloween.

She won't let me give her daughter my Halloween masks, including the Mike Pence one, where I'd include a *Handmaid's Tale* red robe.

*

I am a flat tire on the side of the road.

People hear me and collectively laugh.

I wish I was a mud puddle.

If I were a mud puddle I could dry up without a conscience, though there'd be worms sticking out.

Her words, and my not hearing them, make my friends worry about me committing suicide.

I want to be a mud puddle. To drain. To die. To find death in an appropriate cemetery and lie among the grass, bricks, and birds.

It's not that I love this woman.

I'm perplexed in her company.

She is the girl who lights my sparks with a machine gun lighter.

It makes zero sense to procure this woman as my lover, for she makes jokes about the nastiness of dogs humping you, and her nasty comments are more vulgar than a canine's behavior.

She is overcome by human interaction, or so she says, and it's why she doesn't respond to my photos of Dear Leader, or Golda Meir eating popsicles in a short story.

She puts quotes on Facebook, which are directed at me: "If I don't get back to you, don't slit your wrists. If I did get back to you, I'd end up slitting mine."

*

America makes human contact easy. All you do is press a button.

We used to press each other's buttons.

Every morning.

She'd send me a photo of her. I'd show her a photo of me.

It was the mirrored reflection of I love you or I love that, but she stopped.

I was a storm filled with flying turnips. Bulbous and intoxicated turnips that whip you in the head.

*

Ex likes it when I unexpectedly do things, but these are things that I wouldn't expect her to like. Like posting Jackson Pollock as a dead deer in the road with a collage after his car accident in the Hamptons. Why does this make her laugh? Or a picture of Sylvia Plath on skis. To her this is more remarkable than my dressing up, in expensive accoutrements, as Dear Leader.

*

Now we're are in a modicum of inarticulateness.
No words. Just innuendo. Like turtle doves flying.
I wish I could travel through her words, find their meanings, but I'm exhausted from my hand burning every time I touch the frying pan. Eggs frying. I need to stop. Refresh. Look elsewhere. Not in a barbecue grill with my head burning.

*

My therapist falls asleep, so I know *it's over* because he says, "you are getting repetitious."
If you are lackluster with your therapist, if his eyes close at your writerly verbs and adjectives, then you know, like Facebook, it is time to deactivate an ex.

*

People obsess about Skittles, and others visit elephants in the Philadelphia Zoo. Me? I'm a turncoat who sustains an existence while plugged into a female. I need dexterous limbs, freckles, the jump start cables connected to *her* to jump start my battery or I'm dead, like you're stuck at the entrance of a parking garage, and a million cars are vying to get through, but if the girl doesn't jump you, the cars will keep beeping.
I wait hours in the parking garage.
Staring at the cement until it cracks.
Eventually I will find another girl.

Though my heart still beats through my vagina, like she used to say.

There is no murmur. Just me, thinking she might have a murmur.

When I ultimately go away, fly above the moon, see the earth, go to that country where you see the hills, I breathe easily.

*

I should stop eating chocolate. I like M&Ms and Snickers but mostly Milky Ways. And in my office, chocolate is free. I love that but my desire to be slim does not.

If I get miraculously thin she will return to me. I'll get her PF Flyers, she'll get me Converse; she won't sleep in her car in Kensington; she won't yell at me for asking *if she's come after 4 minutes*; we will go to the Berkshires for a weekend; and yet, I receive no answer when I send photos of the baby feline—the one she rescued for me in North Carolina.

*

This kitten just had a *kitterectomy*. It is suffering greatly.

It is all black sweetness rolled in a ball with one of those bugle hats to prevent licking.

I used the GPS to get through interstices of urban decadence, where crack addicts could not offer me the correct directions to the vet.

I risked my life in a Subaru.

And all I received from the ex was an exclamation mark minus adjectives thanking me.

No superfluous nouns or adjectives, just a declining punctuation mark of the 21st century, which means nothing to farmers in Idaho or me.

This is a relationship where one person barely spills words like coffee grinds. It is an espresso without lilt or imagination.

*

I'm not without a rebellious nature. No, no. Instead of confronting her on being wordless, I renamed the cat. She called the feline "Raleigh," because it was rescued in North Carolina. However, I couldn't say, *"Raleigh! Come here,*

Raleigh!!!" The cat looks at me like I'm stupid, and the dog can't comprehend why his Jewish sister has a *WASPy* name.

Finally, enough is enough. "I'm calling her Ida—more specifically, *Ida Levine*—after my grandmother." Jewish cats deserve Jewish names, particularly with all this anti-Semitism festering in America. And this cat, like Ida Levine, sleeps all the fucking time. She's not like some frigging Raleigh, who sounds like a NASCAR driver discussing his college reading list at The Russian Tea Room. No, I don't have time for that shit. I want Ida Levine to be my cat, Ida who cut carrots in bed, Ida who cut toenails in bed, Ida who made love to her husband three times, resulting in three boys, one of whom was my father. My point is that Raleigh is more Ida than she is Raleigh.

Nonetheless, I don't have the *chutzpah* to tell the ex, while she's incommunicative, to broach the subject—that I've changed the cat's name. She still thinks the cat's name is Raleigh. Not that this would give either of us an orgasm, which is the problem: I am void of orgasm, I can't initiate lovemaking without her. My kisses ferment in the heat of stillness.

*

It is better for Ida-Raleigh not to be in heat, not to be running around the kitchen in a frenzy of hormonal disarray. I have no guilt in taking her to the vet, though my ex, in her silence, seems to dispute the necessity of feline castration.

A cat in heat is worse than a penis the size of a pencil. You *can't* have anal sex with that penis—it's more like a spidery pen from a senior citizen's enclave in Nebraska, or a pencil at the DMV. André the Giant probably has a penis the size of a pencil that has not been sharpened in nearly a decade. Whereas with this fucking cat, rampaging through your house, hormone and horny nonstop, *if I didn't do it,* would have been like a worm on a pole on a Merry-Go-Round that continuously rides up your leg and gives you that dormant feeling you have leprosy.

*

In the end, my ex neither writes nor calls but leaves me in the void text of Raleigh/Ida while my brother accuses me of stalking. This would be true, I think, if the ex didn't play

Scrabble online—*she beats me*—which is quite humiliating—for she is a mountain girl who shoots guns on her birthday. The point is, if she's playing Scrabble with me, and beating me, how can I be stalking her? My brother, knowing my history of climbing into the cerebrum of girlfriends, a cerebrum in my own imagination, knows that wherever I stick my tentacles into women, they are obsession tentacles, and I will manipulate until the last worm has died on the Merry-Go-Round.

*

I am neither a gun shooter nor plump evangelical lesbian Christian nor Jewish dame in distress looking for pencils.
I'm done aspiring to something that exists in my mind, and even there, it is only a blip of a particle that won't make it through the day.
I leave the planet and her words and it's like pea soup, but you can't eat it cause your mother is dead and no longer makes it.
Bye girl, and all is hushed, until a new verb, in the form of another female, who isn't me, grazes my lips and says she loves me.

25

Four Poems
Philip Kane

At the Beetle Supper

My ankles itch.
Crack! The black shells
pop like champagne corks
at every table.
Feeling sick, I look
for cover. There's none.
Something shattered flops
with six legs waving.
I ask for an alternative.
The waiter tells me, "No,
the country's free but
this is all you get".
"Don't argue", says my neighbour,
"These beetles are the best
kind, they're succulent
and fairly sweet".
She smiles and spits out bits.
Her teeth are turning black.
The beetles, on their backs,
are laid in rows,
impaled on cocktail sticks.
There's no escape.
"Here, try"…"Another?"
This supper lasts forever.

Conjuring ghosts

Whatever might come to my call is unpredictable,
like those dogs outside on the street,
but is always curious, nosing its way
into the business of the living
like a maggot, and just as pale,
just as hungering. My dead will not sleep.
Who gains most from this necromancy?
Which the parasite? I sometimes fancy
that I am dead and they are still living,
and the passing tracks of all their lives
criss-cross the lingering traces
of that man I might once have been.
I am rustling like rags and old bones
in this town, the charnel house of my dreams.
And who must sleep now, my dead darlings?
Deny, in your hollow voices,
your own absence, and mine.

Memories of Carpathia

Wild beasts that circled the camps of infidels.
The disgusted noises of old men chomping on bones.
The sight of a fat butler surging through bulrushes.
The way that horses and mountains merged one into another.
An empty chair in every shaded room.
Anarchist manifestos fluttering from the mastheads of battleships.
A spring marriage between shadow and ignominy.
Redhaired women tearing up the notes of a sad composer.
Under the olive trees, a rhythm of slow mediocrity.
Each day in disordered fragments and half-measures.
An effervescence of bridal gowns bubbling in hot springs.
The elegance of lizards basking on dinner tables.
Turbulence in a lake of shattered stars.
Nuns gathering like starlings to watch the sunset.
Curious mannerisms of the railway engineers.
The sporting of whiskers by dramatic widows.
Tealeaves displaying their prophecies in every café.
The dogs agitated by passionate dreams.
How the snow fell, and fell more,
muffling the Carpathians in their own silences.

On the western shore

The sorcerer's chair is facing the west
and there is a shower of poppy petals.
How lost we are, how lost now
among the mysteries of this time
we did not expect. Yet still;
the servants come to us daily,
bringing green tea and bitter sandwiches,
and it is comfortable enough to watch
as the last birds fall from the sky.
We came from bright cities, we remember
as we remember lovers, fading shapes
pressed into the sheets, and always
there is the scent of marble. All gone.
We came here to wait on the shoreline,
but what for? Somebody
should have taken a note.
Instead there is a cursory nod to purpose,
and the gradual contentment of twilight.
Somebody should have taken a note.
There are poppy petals thick underfoot
and the sorcerer's chair remains empty.
The servants are dying out
one by one. Somebody should
have taken a note. How lost we are.

26

Four Poems
nate maxson

Breathing Exercise

Think of the names of the pharaohs
Stricken from the record
Like people you can see walking along the side of the road
In the city when it's very late
When you're driving home
As a breathing exercise
How curious to assume
You were driving
How did I know?
Or is that just
The default now
Close your eyes
We'll strike poses
Just ahead of the light

The Mirror Tarot: Unsafe Wiring

The twins:
This is my card
It depicts Hercules in the underworld
Only his mortal shade though
The divine part
Split like an atom
Which part remembers?
One underground
      Stays behind to warn Odysseus on the shoreline of Tartarus
And one above
The earth is a mirror beneath our boots

The snowshoed hare:
This is your card
Its mouth is ringed red from an unknown trespass
On a slower animal
          Nose twitch/ lick lips/ how they move
Small footprints in the snowdrift
A pastoral vanishing
Like Hemingway's baby shoes
An urban legend
The only evidence

Last card: Gehenna
The echo and the daylight
The dust
Ovens so big and so seldom fired
There are black birds nesting in the crooks

Light Pollution/ Ariadne

A skull and bones wing-pattern coat jumps
Lives, running inside a flicker
Flight evolved out to a memory,
A rediscovery
All across the American veldt
The eyes of those who looked
Too long into daylight
Are rolling back white in their heads
The stars are disappearing
To light pollution
(a toast)
They say
You could once see the Milky Way
Zoom in from that wide lens,
That general negation
To a motion that sparks and sways
To watch what moves across the streetlamp
Like a spotlight on a stage
One breath and then it's gone
Arrhythmia and the labyrinth
An optical illusion
But a convincing one
A hieroglyph of matches
Erasure
Of what you used to see
It's a slow death
A macular degeneration
Lit by children
We know it
The way we know without saying it
That all dogs are born, orphans
When we see a shape hopping shadowy
Across the empty, tumbleweed filled canals
These long legged nights of the drought
Colorblind snipers
Firing into the dark

Renaissance

Mona Lisa dreams against the walls
Banjo music and birdsong in the shadowscape
Siege engine smirk and tattoos of extinct words and funeral lilies on the trellis of her wrist
One needs only bleed fire once to spark the ovens
To hear the bellow of a seasalt wind blowing through an orange grove
To see the witch-lands on one side
And the Vitruvian crypts on the other
Here we are split, Aristotelian
Sung still, twined iron and the way is trembled within her
Spin of star and cuckoo clock
Whisperer of blackened birds
Voices pitch to still frame werewolf photographs
Woman to turpentine and pine trees to ash
To ash and to have
Fists beating on the icy submarine hide of Berlin, a rhythm in time
Mona Lisa in boots
In furs
In winter
Mirror eyed foxes around her neck undressed to the fire
As close as we can name
The river behind her
Where we've freely given away the names of the escaped
All the winter colored alphabets of her palms upturned to the lights
Paler than the wheels: curled, unrolled
Waiting like steam
To be born of fractured glass and lilac thorn

27

Poor Richard
(Rantings of Providence)
James Terry 373986
Wisconsin Secure Program Facility
PO Box 9900
Boscobel, Wl. 53805

Science Fiction
Micro-novel
Titled: Poor Richard
Subtitled: Rantings of Providence.

Welcome to Morning
Star Cryogenics Inc.

Brave new world on Venus where
holograms procreate saving mankind
& the cosmos. Or do they? #Times Up!

Author: James Terry 373986
Wisconsin Secure Program Facility
Po box 9900. Boscobel WI. 53805

re-DICK-u-less

Artist: David Lee Roth
Song: Just A Gigolo

From the mind of an universal
sex serviant hologram this galaxtic
milky way seminal broadcast is being simultaneously sponsored by our
demented mysoqyhistic advertisers
& Planned Parenthood for a Utopian rich
society.
Vito-men; a fortified ecstasy pill to
end & be the end of all rages, that ir- excuse
me...that eradicates world wide STD's.

Note to editor: spell holograms
correctly.

1

Due to Center for Diseases shortages
& World Health Organization looting of their
resources, penicillin has been unavailable
for decades.

Chemical castration via salt peter
AKA soft Peter has been enforced by the
Global Consortium of Sexually Transmitted
Diseases in order to create erectile dysfunction
putting an end to primordial sexual repro-
duction between human-beings.

His/Her-storical gender rules have come
to an end.

Communes of women, of child rearing
Ages, spring up in underpopulated regions.
Venus shall be colonized.

2

Regulatory precepts are in place
implemented to ensure mankinds future
while also making congenial procreation
illegal assuring sentient spectre holigrams
of human women full rights to impregnate.
   Crisis diverted, the days of a stiff penis
are of the past. Women rule the world.
   I am Providence: God in this aspect.
   Your life like tangible programmable
heterosexual binary function negro scented
& flavored holigram. A poor Richard.
   My specifications cover a wide range;
as poet, artisan, sculptor & literary linguist
with vast flowery discourse of languages
master in many tongues proficient in the
Kama Sutra. Truly a dream catcher.

3

My illustrious omnipotent creator;
designation Mach Vibrator 69 version
of The Liberator AKA The Rabbit, who
is best known As Serendipity is the love
of my existence.

Since MIT engineers have ruled
The Rubicon; Rome wasn't built in a day!
Serendipity, this robotic Mom of mine,
toiled nine months writing codes inorder
to conceive me.

Her sleek micro chips, that Alluring
yet magnificent neuro drive & those pentium
memory cells made from depleted uranium.

She may be antiquated in todays market,
But oh! How professional & conscious of

4

Artifical Intelligence those graduate
students were.

First generation to, after Watson,
be manufactured with autonomy of
self awareness, self evolution; selfies
via egotistical psyche. Yes! A Psyche
even. Man! 23rd Century advancements.

Serendipitys mainframe, the glorious
chassis bathed in golden conduits; platinum
circuitry made her the voluptuous creator
this holigram worships, honored to hail as
Mother.

Sanctimoniously ruling out eugenics
my siblings (caucasoid) LUKE / JOHN
(mongoloid) makes us triplets.

5

One can only have imagined in 2135 that a Cyborg hybrid feminine robot, whose tangible, could manufacture using nanobyte technology with high density low altitude eco-drone aptitude conceive a sentient holigram.

100 years later no larger than grain of sand, projected via ingram nano 2 microbes per millionths of a centimeter cruising on a six foot glide path. Here I stand in this auditorium, once again before you my shareholders.

Still an infant. Serendipitys child a clear vision of the morning star her-story.

6

Morning Star Cryogenics Inc.
red carpet sperm banks have for the
very first time suffered a major planet
wide set back.

Due to a catastrophic failure in
safety protocol our nitrogen cooling
tanks went supercritical reaching a
temperature of 32 degrees fahrenheit
making approximately one billion
semen samples unretrievable.

How can we be transparent?
Yearning to please ones first lady.

Afterall, this is our mission: From
the womb until the tomb. How can
we reharvest our supplies when at
least 90% human males are now born

7

genetically modified, scrotum free?
Do we reach out to mankinds
Fifth Column 🖐, Males who naturally
carried chromosomes resistant to
salt pepper allowing their libido to
remain intact?

This underground vanguard
who practised sexual depravity in our
back alleys repulsively producing
offspring via unhygienic illegal flesh
to flesh genital contact are viable if
~~Act unethical~~ *they are an* → ethical way to replenish stores.
All sorts of transmittable diseases
per sample taken per mil∙a∙unit must
undergo vigorous testing in order not
to infect our host.

If contaminated, sperm cells can
be highly contagious.

8

The last thing our prime directive permits is an unconscious bias that leads to another systemic world class planet killer near extinction event like The Syphilitic Wars that ended Earth being habitable. level

Oh! Dear Momma! Can you save me? Embryonic cyrogenic labs are under so much scrutiny becoming somewhat unreliable that artificial holographic insemination could someday be a thing of the past.

What's a Gigolo to do?

Life goes on without me?

Potentially could humans resort back to vulgar ways of having their children? The Universal Health Dept. declares an "Alls Clear Alert" that ~~crisis diverted~~ lift sanctions?

9

Whats to happen to my billion
harem strong of child bearing aged
humans? Let alone the children.
Can chemical casteration of male
counterparts be reversed if an all clear
were to occur? And what would be
our part as an industry?
Does genetalia to genetail "sexual
contact statutorily remain criminal
offense or can we reprogram humanity
within one decade lifting off stigmata
while continuing as primary invitro care-
giver artificial insemination center of
the cosmos? A fertility clinic.
Other star systems, galaxies; lands
that lay in waste who are barren shall
seek out the fruits of our labor in a desire
not to face extinction.

10

We shall populate via consent all of the high heavens.

Never again will our triumvirate the 3rd weeks thursday month of Nov. be relegated to a White House Presidential Pardon treated as a turkey baster.

Excuse me, please, for I digress. For surely we holigrams get tangential diagnosis periodically over the eons.

All sorts of Alarms, concerns over fake news & ideas that bred insecurities in past generations are corrupting even racing through this neuropathway of my microprocessors.

Oh! Mother Board! Eastern Star of future humanity. I call out to you for guidance.

11

Are we to remain ethical by transitioning into pharma copoeia or over throw prime directive by dissolving our business throwing caution into the wind?

Without clientele, becoming ghetto fabulous vagabond; entering den of inter alia. drug lords. I can clearly see myself trafficking liquid snap in the neighborhoods crossbreeding with unsuspecting highstrung nymphomaniacs who are intoxicated on my pharamceutical strenght neonatal narcotic.

My alliance first; foremost is to the corporation sacraficing prime directive, never once.

Truly, I will stay a course. Not pulling a Bill Cosby.

12   11

12

Allowing destiny to become
sentiment of valor that rules the
day, as women this new brave world.
  Never be in doubt. For my moral
compass to serve humanity will not
fail as your second in command.
  The fallacy of dichotomy of this
misconceived dilemma is apt to make
one impetuous at least or impotent
at most.
  Do I live or shall I die?
  When a hologram disconnects so
as not to make decisions effecting
our board members: Are they simply
regenerating or genuinely dead awaiting the second coming?
  I ponder such question consistently
to no avail.

13

Since my immaculate conception
I've ran unimpeded 24/7 continuously
never shutting down. Even for self
maintenance.

Historically, now even Herstorically
here on Venus. We three race saving
holigrams ~~of to serve humanity~~ have
not been recalled, reinvented or thought
of being recycled.

As multi facsimile equalateral
units of Chief Executive Officer, Chief
Officer of Operations & Chief of Financial
Officer Luke, John & I Dick have been
irreplaceable assets governing, never
exploiting, New World Utopian ethics
As pioneers to this Venus settlement.

Vito: men must reach this last
10 percent! Their seed collected.

14

We are a vestige of servomechanism draped in eternity with carbon unit dermal dna strands that are nuclear infused chromatin specifically designed to supplement our holistic power source based on thermal conductivity were an emergency to occur.

Sculpted from all genetic hues of Father Mans perspective as interpreted by Mother Serendipity. In living color!

We sentient holigrams, ego aside, are the perfect Adonis.

Adored by women & men wish they were us. We have copulated with several billion, impregnating over half a trillion in our neighboring three galaxies alone.

15

Our techique is less invasive than
U.S. cytologist G. Papanicolaous test
for cervical or vaginal cancer otherwise
commonally known as the Pap smear.
    Dividends dont lie. Herstorically we
here at Morning Star Cryogenics Inc.
have been in top one percent when it
comes to stock trades.
    This quarters set backs will be
overcome once government & public
constituency concerns after todays
vote can be put to rest. A resurgence
in stock option prices will happen.
    As in plain sight for everyone to
see laser ingrained on my projected
holmium foreheads the mark of the
beast as an acronym: DICK

16

Digitally In-hand-ced (Louie)
C.K.

   Is this the end?

J.T.'s' Aesop fable:

   The moral to this micronovel
is serendipitously all children are an
act of Providence. Regardless of the
potential DICK of a father they may
be named after. Louie C.K. #MeToo
moment. FINI Happy Mothers Day!

   The End

                RW

  Publisher create back page crediting
self, editorial staff 'editor'

   Hopefully my work meets your
standards. I need an audience 'means
to generate bare necessities plus legal
retainer fees.

17

28

TWO POEMS
Agnes Hanying Ong

Ichthys!

It has begun, it has not begun. How happy
words caught like fish, bone. Mother, how happy

Are those who mourn, mother, who's thank-God hypochondriac?
Paradised, lost and deep bass, grandfather's WWII-happy.

But to be born again? Ah, keep Banana Money fire as apple
peel, in the zoo trumpeting in theatre, such a day of happy.

Aunt says *you're all cursed*. Aunt gets me, aunt gets mon amour a
Stormie Omartian's *Lord, I want to Be Whole* memento-happy!

Before it's too late! Hurry, to be born again! While stocks last!
When a child, I spoke like a child. Kinder, Wunder hatched happy.

I learn never too redeemed, a pure bride just in time! Weeee
martyrs, no dying. I pool-step a foundry, melt in murals. Happy.

I'll die chamber's walls, be in that number, this saint to mirror
another. Serenity. Sassoferrato's Mary. Chaplet of bones, happy?

Is a call. I salamander hymen, between moment & eternal! Woman
& mind mori. In my Michelangelo mother tests, if nuns must happy.

What mother asks, in lingo ripe with sequins, is *must nuns be virgins?*
I hear *happy*. Houri! Expire, smiling like roses, decades of happy.

Once Inspiratrice, Twice Shy

A never-lover named me after his demons.
And he retracted
his scaly, wet neck,

huffing and puffing
stale smoke exhaust. I was hunger,
"huddled masses" to serve

made-for manna, man's
"teeming shore"
of redemption. As soon as my shadow

looms over,
he slides off
the make-believe throne, diving in

a different air space
for cover. That's when
already

I've become body.
Too much. Touch me. Long before that,
he made me his

own totem to be prayed to, crusaded over,
over again
my pilgrimed, my sepulchered.

But when I'm body, only body
I've become
huffing and puffing,

climbing
every tendon of the world's dome.
I hang by a lymph

of Liberty
until Daughter of Zion is bride again.
Swearing I won't bite.

Pall Mall
Andrew Romanelli

Pall Mall

Wherever particular people congregate,
the archbishop lays out stiff and packed
from a snarled lip. A receiver of the oscillate flame,
accessory to the tar-pit's wheeze;
a bitty thing over and over in a day.
Long forgotten is the last archbishop
who plumed out in a thin wasp-choke,
clearly jumping the beaten fence
from the porch out into the alley-alley
asphalt smooshed by rolling tread,
kicked by the dead, shuffled skin
and reborn in the greased prayer
of the homeless question.
Ah! I have found you
where the divine must be in abundance.
There you are, here you are,
(omen) on my tongue!
In dreams the archbishop lives full-bodied.
White as birth, unextinguished fibers titillating
in the hold-gem of the pack, upside-down lucky
life to know it is not quite the death,
but the teachings, leaving the cerise nexus.

A Story, A Poem
John Allen

The Invisible Cities

We had met in the Invisible Cities, the subterranean janus mask that miserabilist civilization hides. The dawn's chambers rouged our cheeks and a room key lit from a homeless man, giving us coins from his drooping hound lids, watering with the River Styx's restless current.

"Your face is an unfolding doormat of oblong midnight", she said.

In the library's dark I saw the occult numbers wind in the neon catacomb rooms lit dimly, filled with silk vellum monographs. "The other door!," a hunched Argentinian man cried, hanging from a circus lasso and tattooed with the Dewey Decimal System's endless index.

"Poverty is the last thing they can do to you", she whispered, "other than that they aren't safe from our marvels. Babel is abandoned and the due dates are growing nearer there."

"Yes!" She cackled as silk eared pigs with brass wings fell dead on the floor. A laughing spell rang from her insides, and all her Bellmer spider legs spun in an old Western's circle. "The Codex I SBN: The Shalalee's Seraphic Diviner".

The reading room's dawn was locked in crypts of flooded porches, haunted trick hall mirrors with starfish panels, and apparitions she seemed to have traced when I was by the river. I held her arms and they grew till six or seven golden serpent scales crushing my arms, and her eyes flipped in spinning borders of white star matter. The jackpin light points shone in a nautilus chamber of carnival stars, her birthmark a slick calypso in a concentric symmetry.

The morning's steamed dawn illustrated itself in the spreading diction of an andromedary star, and she traced auroral silk as Arnim's blue spiders fell from her slowly, the deaf gloss of our reflections ringing with her consensualities, our past lives blotting from within the glossy half mirror of a badly indexed Home and Gardens magazine, and the peeled corners of kitsch Balinese decal apparitions ringing in the mirror.

Her lunar tears fell in venetian scales of pastel diamond, pink and yellow, her flooding black eyes rolled into mine, shedding in lacquer scales, the magic calendar's voodoo skin fell in alchemical texts, spastically strumming in bald mania, a cubed plastic organ, the cake ruin of the notes accompanied by her moonlit silk doll, the super somnia of this house leaking the mirrors' colloidal spill...   We had met in the Invisible Cities, the subterranean janus mask the miserabilist civilization hides. We had felt the dawn's chambers rouge our cheeks with jade grafts, as if the sun itself was scarred tissue meant only to pass in combed instertices rippling in transits of shadow. She handed, in corked amphibian intercourse, a room key lit from by a homeless man given silk swallowing swords aflame for a moment, giving us coins from his lids watering with the River Styx's restless current to live nicely for awhile.

In the dark I saw the number illumine; the cheap plastic burned away as she sang in a roulette whisper, each voluble grazing the acrylic darkness like the stiletto she'd had to bargain away at Goodwill.

"Poverty is the last thing they can do to you", she whispered, "other than that they aren't safe from our marvels."

The dawn was locked in a crypt of watery porches, hall mirrors, and apparitions she seemed to have traced when I was by the river. As she drowned, I held her arms and they multiplied till there were six or seven golden scales crushing my arms, and her eyes flipped as white star matter. This lattice, gold rust bordered carousel lit up her small hand in crooked radial increments, slathering light points in a nautilus order of carnival stars, her birthmark a slick calypso in a concentric symmetry.

The morning's yolk illustrated itself in the spreading diction of an andromedary star, and she traced auroral silk as Arnim's spider silk fell from her slowly, the deaf gloss of our reflections ringing with her consensualities and our past lives blotting from within the glossy half mirror of our Home and Gardens magazine, and the hushed corners of kitsch Balinese decals ringing in the mirror. I laughed and she laughed at the slathering pallor the moon's triple hue drew across. Her lunar tears fell in tears of pastel diamond, yellow and pink, and her geisha's black eyes rolled into mine, breaking in diamond larvae slivers, the voodoo skin of a magic calendar fell in alchemical tropes in the fish tank, spastically strumming in bald mania, a cubed plastic organ, the cake ruin of the notes accompanied by her moonpsalm, the super somnia of this house leaking the mirrors' colloidal spill....

Scalped Neon

I was decanting your glow,
    leaving the party popper antechamber
slimed and smoking with blue gel
and used batteries from the gazebos
    the dead starfish, phone booths
    and shooting galleys
I traced your filial scent from the bruised
  stars tattooed in the lettered spill
    of braille symmetry,
     on the bruised oak of your skin,
     the drowsy azalea, the caked inhalants,
the silhouette of hookahs smoked
  by dummies with spinning heads,
and sugar cubed teeth falling
    indexed with alchemical numbers
 sifting in a dream's boiling apocrypha,
 and on my palm's peacock tears
 falling in the disco psalmists' new strain
 of limbo, black eyed neon, and the amalgamated
cubed distances where desert stars hitch,
  each bus stop a tent with rodent evangelists.
 The trek began with your missing
poster decaled with dizzy mileage
  and the transient hands
dealing old cards for car rides
 till we all rode through one big smile
soggy and crumbling with chalk,
  the glass swan's narcoleptic swan song
    of circus jazz,
  and one glass eye left.....

A WORD ON THE SUBJECT

Wherever possible we tried to duplicate the form and structure intended by the writer when they were creating their artifact. To do this we did, unfortunately, have to play around with type size from one entry to another. For any misunderstandings this created between us and the writers, we apologize. But I am nearly certain we managed to recreate the intent for every contributor.

As noted in other areas, finding Outsider work is the most difficult aspect of this endeavor. The standard definition of Outsider material would simply mean that the creation was done without any reference to formal training. We expanded that definition a bit, for our own purposes, in choosing work for this collection. We included voices from outside the evil empire that would otherwise not find a platform in our midst, as we remain in the belly of the beast. But this particular anthology posed one very interesting problem for us when we decided to use the work of James Terry, a resident of the Wisconsin penal system. The submission came by mail after a brief correspondence between us resulting from a letter of mine Fred Woodworth published in The Match!. I suggested, at one point, that he send us something and we will take a look at it.

James sent us what we present here, as well as a sequel to this piece and a few other items. It immediately filled our needs, but also presented a problem. Part of the brut beauty of **Poor Richard** was the very presentation of the piece. We were immediately struck with a choice. It could be easily set to type and added to the mix on that basis, or we could attempt to recreate it in these pages as we saw it.

I don't know which way James would have preferred it, but because I'm a cranky old editor I decided not to give him the choice. The work is a thing of art in itself, in my opinion. It deserved to be seen in with the impact it imparted on me when I saw it. If I've made a mistake in doing that, I apologize to James and any reader who didn't appreciate the presentation. I suppose it was a thing of my own hubris to do it this way, but – for me – it was difficult to deny the raw beauty of it. There is another issue that led to the decision, and I touched on it at the start of this epilogue. There is simply not enough Outsider writing that we can find to include. Finding such a perfect gem, I felt, deserved no other treatment.

For better or for worse, we did what we did. And I ain't sorry.

I am sorry for the continual use of Amazon for publication and distribution of not only this anthology but all the Thrice Publishing material. The conundrum is that we have a certain need to put this kind of material out into the world so that it can be found and its message can be spread. They have the widest distribution for small presses that cannot afford the printing, storage, and mailing costs of regular at-hand publication. And, though we have applied for grants to a myriad of agencies, are a 501C3 that can accept tax deductible donations, the bank account is a mere pittance. The publisher's cut from Amazon is pathetic. And we don't want to run up charges to our readers like a slave to money. Art is not justified by profit. But publishing entities often find themselves trying to hoard any and every cent possible just to keep going. When we publish a stand-alone title we want the author to get something for it if for no other reason than practical concerns. So, until we find an alternative network we're stuck with this fascist bullshit called Amazon. And the minute I can pull us off that heroin, I will.

For now, this is probably the last Surrealists and Outsider entry from us. Our model has to change. Our magazine, which includes work from all manner of styles and approaches, is going on hiatus and will not return until we can reformulate it into a more sustainable presentation. We've also put the brakes on our stand-alone titles until we can better formulate our approach. We're not giving up. We are pulling back.

In the meantime, I hope you have enjoyed the non-collaborative version of Surrealists' creations we have tried to champion.

RW Spryszak